"I love a romance popu... truly root for. And this one has that and more. Coupled with Toni Shiloh's winning voice, it's a story not to be missed."

Oprah Daily on *In Search of a Prince*

"This romance with a touch of mystery will stay with you long after The End."

Rachel Hauck, *New York Times* bestselling author, on *In Search of a Prince*

"Toni Shiloh brilliantly weaves a romantic tale."

Vanessa Riley, bestselling author of *Island Queen*, on *In Search of a Prince*

"Shiloh has penned yet another adorable and charming royal romance!"

Melissa Ferguson, bestselling author of *Meet Me in the Margins*, on *To Win a Prince*

"Shiloh offers a sweet romance with a strong dose of spiritual truth."

Pepper Basham, award-winning author of *Authentically, Izzy*, on *The Love Script*

"Toni Shiloh delivers another soulful, uplifting romance. . . . A swoon-worthy romance readers will adore."

Belle Calhoune, bestselling author of *An Alaskan Christmas Promise*, on *The Love Script*

"Another winner that readers will enjoy from start to finish."

Vanessa Miller, author of *Something Good*, on *To Win a Prince*

"Shiloh delivers a fun, contemporary romance delightfully full of favorite romantic tropes that also conveys serious messages of faith and destiny. It is refreshing to see dynamic Black characters in the genre, and readers will be eager for this modern-day fairy tale."

Library Journal starred review of *In Search of a Prince*

You Make It
Feel like
Christmas

You Make It Feel like Christmas

TONI SHILOH

BETHANYHOUSE

a division of Baker Publishing Group
Minneapolis, Minnesota

Published by Bethany House Publishers
Minneapolis, Minnesota
www.bethanyhouse.com

Bethany House Publishers is a division of
Baker Publishing Group, Grand Rapids, Michigan

Printed in the United States of America

Library of Congress Cataloging-in-Publication Data
Names: Shiloh, Toni, author.
Title: You make it feel like Christmas / Toni Shiloh.
Other titles: I'll be home
Description: Minneapolis, Minneapolis : Bethany House Publishers, a
division of Baker Publishing Group, [2023]
Identifiers: LCCN 2023002711 | ISBN 9780764242267 (casebound) | ISBN
    9780764242069 (paperback) | ISBN 9781493443789 (ebook)
Subjects: LCGFT: Christmas fiction. | Romance fiction. | Christian fiction. | Novellas.
Classification: LCC PS3619.H548 I45 2023 | DDC 813/.6—dc23/eng/20230123
LC record available at https://lccn.loc.gov/2023002711

Previously published in 2019 under the title *I'll Be Home*.

Emojis are from the open-source library OpenMoji (https://openmoji.org/) under the
Creative Commons license CC BY-SA 4.0 (https://creativecommons.org/licenses/by
-sa/4.0/legalcode)

Cover design by Jennifer Parker

The author is represented by the Rachel McMillan Agency.

Baker Publishing Group publications use paper produced from sustainable forestry
practices and post-consumer waste whenever possible.

23   24   25   26   27   28   29   7   6   5   4   3   2   1

To the Author and Finisher of my faith

❄ *one* ❄

S tarr Lewis hated to return home a failure, but at least she had the cover of the holiday season to hide her embarrassment.

The wind whipped through her as she stepped off the train. She shuddered and drew her coat closed at the neck, then followed her fellow passengers up the escalator to the main building. The man in front of her held the door open, and she trailed in behind him. Warmth caressed her face in a greeting, chasing the chill away.

She sighed and took a moment to admire the arched ceiling over Union Station. People hurried around her as she made her way toward the front doors. Her brother Gabe was picking her up, which meant she'd have thirty minutes to kill until he showed up. Gabe was always late. *Always.*

Starr tightened her grip on the handle of her fuchsia carry-on and headed for Jamba Juice. A mix of passion fruit, mango, and strawberry would be just the thing to freeze out the hot shame of returning home jobless.

Who cared if she'd had a smoothie before leaving New York

City? One could never have too many. Besides, she needed the liquid goodness to chase away reminders of being laid off and forced to live in her childhood bedroom for who knew how long. Out of the five Lewis children, Starr was the only one who no longer held an illustrious career.

Shake it off. You're not a failure. This is just a setback.

Of epic proportions. Not only did she have to move back home, but her demise lined up perfectly with her sister Angel's Christmas Eve wedding. To Starr's ex-boyfriend. *Ugh. God, please help me. I'm not sure how I'll make it through the wedding without wanting to gag.*

The hits just kept on coming. She'd better order a large smoothie.

Kelly Clarkson's rendition of "I'll Be Home for Christmas" crooned through the speakers. Starr shook her head at the unnecessary reminder and slowed as she got in line at Jamba Juice. Her cell buzzed in her coat pocket. She moved off to the side, pulling out the pink-encased iPhone and checking the caller ID. "Where are you?"

"Calm down. I'm on Union Station Drive with all the taxis and tourists. Should I park around back, or can you come out front?"

Her bottom lip poked out as dreams of smoothie bliss evaporated. "I'll be out front in a sec."

"Don't sound so enthused."

"I'm just a little hungry."

"You mean hangry? Well, grab some food then. But keep in mind I'm taking up space, and security might be giving me the side-eye—"

"All right, I get it," she snapped. The moment Gabe had said he was at the front entrance, she'd started walking that way.

Starr exited through the double doors and searched the cars lined up in front of her. "Are you in your car?"

"Dad's. My car died last week."

She sighed in relief when she spotted the familiar black Mercedes. "I see you." She headed his way, dragging her carry-on behind her.

"I see you too." Gabe popped out of the driver's door and came around the passenger side as he pocketed his phone. "Sis!" He picked her up, twirling her around.

She chuckled at his exuberance. "Put me down." Her head spun, but she soon caught her bearings. As she peered into Gabe's familiar features a pang twinged in her chest. Gabe was probably her favorite sibling. Her older brother also had the smoothest skin she'd ever seen. Probably beat out women who held a daily regimen of wrinkle-free cream and exfoliation. He definitely fit into the pretty-boy category.

"Did you miss me?" He waggled his eyebrows, then grabbed her suitcase.

"Maybe." Her lips twitched.

"Yeah, you did." He winked at her and closed the trunk. "Don't stand there all day. Mom and Dad are holding Thanksgiving dinner just for you."

Thank goodness. She was starved. She slid onto the passenger seat and buckled her seat belt. "That explains why I didn't have to wait too long."

"Ha." He shrugged. "What can I say? Life is meant to be enjoyed, not hurried."

"No one says you have to rush for everything. Just be on time for what's important."

"Like picking up my little sister?" He tossed an amused expression her way before turning to look at the road.

"Exactly." She slid her frozen hands under her thighs. "It's so cold here. It wasn't even this cold in New York."

"Oh, look at me," Gabe said in a high-pitched voice. "I just came from New York, and like"—he flipped his imaginary long hair— "I'm such a cosmopolitan now. DC is beneath me and all that I know."

She smacked his arm. "I'm just making a weather observation."

"For now."

Same ol' Gabe. She rolled her eyes. "How's everyone?"

"The same. Noel is going to work himself into an early grave. Eve is following in his footsteps, and Angel is Angel." He shrugged as he navigated through DC traffic.

Wreaths hung about the city streetlights as they had every Christmas since Starr could remember. She couldn't help the smile that tilted her lips. "It's good everything's the same."

"Is it?"

"Sure." Well, maybe the physical things. She didn't want to walk in the house and have everyone treat her like the baby just because she was the youngest Lewis sibling. She wanted to be taken seriously, but losing her job wouldn't add points in that direction.

"I'm surprised your boss gave you such a long break. Mom said you don't have to go back until the day after New Year's. Is that right?"

"Yep. Nice, huh?" Though it wasn't a vacation but her being handed a severance package and two letters of recommendation.

But that tidbit was her secret.

Starr had packed her household goods into a storage unit before leaving the city and returning to DC. If she was smart with her money, she could pay for the unit for four months. Obviously, she'd have to come clean to her parents well before then. If she was still here in the springtime, there was no way her folks would believe she'd been given that long of a vacation. Then again, maybe telling them she was working remotely would help her save face.

That's lying.

She tensed. Hopefully by the end of the month, she'd find another job, and they'd be none the wiser.

"Suspiciously nice."

Starr looked at Gabe, hoping she was projecting a calm demeanor that belied the fast beating of her heart. "The company values their employees."

Only she hadn't been one of them. Layoffs had to happen, and someone had to go. Why not the hardworking PR associate who saved more butts than the others? She'd only worked for the company for two years, which meant she was the easiest to say good-bye to.

Story of her life.

Her ex, Ashton, had had no trouble saying good-bye after taking one long look at Angel.

"I see." Gabe met her gaze, raising an eyebrow in skepticism. "You know you can talk to your big brother, right? Tell me your worries. Your *secrets.*"

"I don't have any." She faced straight ahead, looking out the windshield, then gasped and leaned forward. "Is it snowing?"

"Just a few flakes. They didn't even salt the roads, so it's nothing."

"Or we'll get a bigger snowfall than expected and be trapped at home." She did *not* want to be trapped at home with all her siblings to poke their noses in her business.

"Works for me. I don't want to go to work tomorrow anyway."

Starr snorted. "Working for your parents is *so* difficult."

"Don't be jealous. You know Dad would give you a job if you wanted."

"I do *not* want to work in finance." She hated math. Had *always* hated math and had the grades to reflect that. Too bad everyone else in the family was a math genius.

Even Angel.

Lord, I pray that I hold up seeing Angel again. After all, she didn't intentionally steal my boyfriend. She's just . . . Angel.

A selfish, manipulative—

No, no. She really didn't think Angel was aware of how Starr truly felt. After all, Starr hadn't called her names or threatened bodily harm. After introducing her boyfriend to her sister, Starr had later listened incredulously as Angel described her meeting with Ashton as fate in some star-crossed-lover-type drama. Apparently, Ashton felt the same way. He dumped Starr so he could ask Angel out and live happily ever after.

Starr sighed.

"What's going on in that head of yours?"

"I was just wondering what the holidays will be like." She offered a stiff smile. "You know how Mom is."

Gabe grimaced. "Unfortunately. My prediction is full-on Christmas drama with an extra helping of wedding chaos thrown in."

Just what she feared. "Great."

"Hey, you wanted to come back. You didn't seem to mind missing the last couple of Christmases." Gabe glanced at her. "Why break the streak now?"

"Angel's getting married." As much as she had hurt Starr, Angel was still her sister.

"True, but you could've come down the day before and left after Christmas Day. No need to torture yourself the whole holiday season."

Except now Starr had nowhere else to go. Her severance package wouldn't have lasted long in New York. Staying with her parents would give her time to plan her next steps. Only, she couldn't let anyone know that.

She pushed aside her feelings and pasted on a smile. "I missed you guys."

Gabe snorted. "You mean your friends."

"What?" She gasped. "I love all of you guys."

"You never hung around us growing up."

"Well, it's not my fault Noel and Eve were so much older. They've always had their own friends." Sometimes being born last was the pits. Starr had been lonely until she took matters into her own hands.

"True. But you didn't hang with me and Angel either."

"That's because you had your twin superpowers activated and didn't let anyone else in the club."

Gabe took advantage of the red light to give Starr a long look, confusion written all over his face. "Is that really how you felt?"

"It's the truth."

"Starr . . ." He sighed and hit the gas. The car lurched forward. "We never meant to exclude you."

"I get it. I'm the fifth and last kid. Everyone had already paired off by the time I could talk and play. I had to make my own friends in order to have some, not because I didn't love my family."

"I'm sorry, Starr."

She shrugged and looked out the passenger window. The Lewis family liked to portray themselves as close-knit, but she'd always been on the outside looking in. She didn't expect the holidays to change that. And Angel's wedding definitely wouldn't.

Maybe she'd be able to reconnect with some of her friends who still lived in the area. Anything to occupy her days and keep the melancholy at bay.

"I'll make it up to you, 'kay?"

"How?" She peeked at Gabe.

"You can hang out with me and my friends."

"Really, Gabe? I'm a little too old for the 'kid sister tagging along with the older brother' bit."

"You'll like them."

We'll see. "I'm sure."

He grinned, his straight teeth a testament to the years he'd worn braces. "Then it's settled."

"First, let's get through dinner."

Gabe turned down their street, and Starr's pulse picked up speed. The neighbors always joined forces to decorate for the Christmas season. She knew this week had been spent decorating the exteriors of the multimillion-dollar homes. Every house glowed with white lights. Starr sank into her seat as their whitewashed brick home came into view. Navy shutters surrounded the candlelit windows, and a silver wreath decorated the matching front door.

"The inside is decked out, isn't it?"

"From top to bottom. Mom decorated all yesterday."

Starr chuckled. Their mom was a little too enthusiastic about Christmas. It's why they all had Christmas names, even though Gabe and Angel were the only ones born in December. Every year, the day before Thanksgiving, her mom would pull out the decorations and play her Christmas music for "atmospheric purposes."

Gabe pulled into the garage, and Starr was out of the car before the garage door could close again.

"I'll grab your bag."

"Thanks, Gabe."

"Mom's probably in the kitchen."

Starr entered the house and headed straight to the kitchen. Her jaw dropped. Gone were the black cabinets and red backsplash. The room seemed bigger with white cabinetry and black fixtures. The sapphire-blue backsplash went with the silver and blue Christmas decorations her mother was fond of.

"Baby girl!" Her mom threw open her arms as she came

around the island and swept Starr into a hug. "Happy Thanksgiving."

"Happy Thanksgiving, Mom."

"I'm so glad you're home. Now all my babies are home." She grinned at Starr and folded Gabe into a group hug.

After a few seconds, she stepped back.

"Gabe said dinner was on hold. I didn't mean to make you guys wait," Starr said.

"Gabe." Her mother's black brows dipped in consternation. "Dinner won't be ready for another thirty minutes." She shook her head. "He's just making trouble."

"Me?" He pointed to his chest in mock horror. "I'm the angel, unlike your middle-born daughter."

"Ha. Go take your sister's suitcase to her room."

"Yes, ma'am." Gabe strolled out of the kitchen with a parting wink to Starr.

"You changed it." Starr gestured around the kitchen. "It looks good, by the way."

"Thank you. Angel brought my ideas to life."

Of course Angel redesigned it.

"But don't worry," her mom continued, "your room is the same as you left it."

Starr paused, her hand in midair with the meatball she'd swiped from the appetizer tray. "You mean, *exactly* the same?"

"Of course. The cleaning staff go in to dust once a month and don't touch anything else."

"But I haven't lived here since college." She'd graduated five years ago and moved to New York shortly after. This was really the first time she'd been back home apart from a visit here and there while staying at hotels—because she could afford to.

"You'll always have a room here, baby. You know that." Her mom dipped her head and shook it at the same time.

Now would be a good time to inform Mom about her unemployed state, but that news could wait. Maybe after the wedding, when everyone returned to their regular schedules. "Is everyone coming to dinner?"

"Of course. Noel will be here straight from work. He said he invited a friend."

"A *girlfriend?*"

Her mother rolled her eyes. "I wish. He's in his thirties, for goodness' sake. How much longer is he going to make me wait for grandchildren?"

"He's married to his work."

"Don't I know it. But ledgers don't produce living, breathing babies." Her mother turned a burner off as she checked on another pot. "Eve is already here. Her condo got flooded from an upstairs neighbor, so she's staying in her old room until the repairs are done."

"That's awful." *Guess I'm not the only one dealing with stuff.*

"It was just *terrible.* She lost everything."

Poor Eve. Starr straightened, then put on her calm façade. "And Angel?"

"Angel and Ashton will be joining us too."

Her stomach dropped. "He—they will?"

"Of course." Her mom gave her an odd look. "Wedding preparations are in full swing, and those two are never out of each other's sight."

Disgusting. What had she subjected herself to? Maybe she should've looked harder for a job in the city. Anything to avoid seeing her ex and sister fall all over each other.

Her mother stilled, her brow furrowing. "You aren't jealous . . . are you?"

"Of course not." Starr put her practiced *as if* expression on. She'd perfected the look in the Amtrak bathroom because she knew someone would ask at some point. "We're old history."

"Well, not that old. It was only two years ago you two were together."

Way to rub the salt in, Mom. "We weren't serious." Well, *he* hadn't been. She hadn't known how serious she'd been until he'd willingly parted ways to go after Angel.

"I didn't think so. You never introduced us to him."

"We lived in different states!" She stared at her mom, shock running through her.

"Oh, sweetie, that won't matter when you meet the right guy. You'll see."

If her mom was going to ignore how Angel and Ashton got together, Starr wouldn't be expecting any sympathy this holiday season. *Welcome home, Starr.* "I think I'll go up to my room."

"Be sure to change into something presentable."

Because her slacks and silk blouse were abhorrent? "Yes, Mother."

"Don't you 'Mother' me. We'll have company. Dress your best."

Of course. That was her mother's motto.

✳ two ✳

Waylon Emmerson adjusted the Windsor knot in the red tie above the V of his black sweater. Mrs. Lewis always required her guests to dress up for dinner, and he was scared enough of her that he'd follow her wishes even though he'd rather throw on a football jersey and sit in front of the TV.

But then he'd be alone for Thanksgiving.

With his sister living overseas in Japan and his mother's recent passing, Waylon found himself adrift. Thankfully, Noel had invited him over to the Lewis household for Thanksgiving dinner. A little time with their crew should take his mind off the red that had begun to creep into his mom's store's—no, *his* store's—ledger. He needed to think of ways to propel the shop to success, but not tonight.

He slid his wallet into his back pocket and grabbed his cell and car keys. Since he lived in Alexandria, it would take him a little while to drive to DC. The metro traffic always annoyed, but holiday traffic was more painful than a tooth in need of a root canal. Maybe everyone would be off the streets and around the dinner table by now, allowing him to get there more quickly than usual.

Traffic, indeed, moved slowly, but it *did* move. Finally, he turned onto the Lewises' street. Every house in the neighborhood shone with white lights outlining the homes. They looked classy and full of holiday cheer. He pulled into the half-circle driveway and parked behind Noel's car.

Waylon adjusted the hem of his sweater as he went up the walkway, then rang the doorbell.

The door swung open, and his breath caught. Noel's youngest sister stood in the entry, an inviting smile gracing her face. Where was the awkward pipsqueak who used to hide around the house? In her place stood a beautiful woman. Her light brown hair fell down her back in big curls, and her black floral dress hugged curves he'd never seen before. Her light brown skin practically glowed. Then again, the shine could be from the foyer lighting. "Starr?"

"Hey, Waylon." She motioned him to enter. "How've you been?"

"Um, good." He cleared his throat and stepped over the threshold. When had Starr become so . . . so . . . *stunning?*

His pulse beat erratically. Since when did his friend's little sister's looks wreak havoc to his insides? "Uh, how are you? I haven't seen you in forever."

"I'm good." She flashed a smile, but something about it seemed forced.

"Are you sure?" he asked softly.

Noel had told him Angel was marrying Starr's ex. Maybe she was hung up on what's-his-face. For some reason, the thought twisted his insides.

"Yes." She nodded, bobbing her head too quickly to be taken seriously. "It's good to be back home."

"I'm glad you're here."

Surprise danced across her features.

"I mean, Noel is. He couldn't stop talking about it."

"Really? I didn't think he'd noticed I was gone."

Waylon leaned against the foyer wall, feigning a nonchalance that was far from accurate. "I think you're his favorite."

"No way." She stepped closer, whispering as if they were conspiring together. "I'm pretty sure Noel wishes you were his real brother."

"Well, Gabe can drive anyone crazy." He chuckled. "But, nah, Noel loves his family."

Skepticism had her brows contorting. "Hmm. Maybe I've been gone too long to recall that particular quality of his."

"What quality?"

Starr whirled around, and Waylon straightened as Noel strode down the hall.

"Are your ears burning?" Starr placed her hands on her hips.

Noel patted his ears. "Should they be?" He bent down and kissed her on the cheek. "Happy Thanksgiving, sis."

"Happy Thanksgiving to you." She gestured to Waylon. "Your friend was revealing all your secrets."

"I wasn't." Waylon slid his hands into his pockets. But if Starr didn't know she was Noel's favorite, then, yeah, he'd inadvertently let a secret slip.

"He better not. I know some of his." Noel grinned.

Starr rubbed her hands in glee. "Do tell."

"First, tell me the secret he told you."

"That I'm your favorite."

Noel made an exaggerated show of searching the halls before looking at Starr. "That's true, but the others can't know." He winked.

"Really? I thought Eve was your favorite."

Did Waylon detect a bit of hope in that statement? He shifted so he could see Starr's expression. Her mouth had parted in surprise. Why did her being the favorite seem so impossible to believe?

22

"Eve's too much like me to be my favorite."

Waylon chuckled.

Starr looked at him with a bemused expression. "Why's that so funny?"

"Because it's true. It's like your mom had two sets of twins, with Noel and Eve leading the way."

"And me stuck by myself."

Something in her tone struck a chord. Was Starr lonely? Did she feel isolated in her own home? Waylon understood loneliness. With his mom gone and sister overseas, Waylon had never felt so alone. Even when Noel offered to hang out, Waylon found himself too introspective to appreciate the company.

Before he could make a comment, the door flew open, and Angel and her fiancé sauntered in.

"We're here!" Angel took off her camel-colored wrap and did a little jig. "Happy Thanksgiving, everyone."

"Happy Thanksgiving, Angel," Noel replied. "Look who else is here." He placed a hand on Starr's shoulder.

"Starr!" Angel flew forward, wrapping her younger sister in her arms. "I'm so glad you're here. This is going to be a great holiday. I just know it." Angel pulled back and beamed.

Waylon couldn't help noting the contrast the two sisters presented. Angel's black hair had been twisted at the nape and fixed with a diamond-encrusted hair comb, her tan satin dress was belted at the waist, and her heels mirrored stilts.

She exuded the air of a socialite, while Starr embodied . . .
Home.

He blinked. Obviously, the holidays had put him in a nostalgic mood.

"Ashton, sweetie, grab us something to drink while I catch up with Starr." Angel fluttered her eyelashes at her fiancé.

Ashton smirked, and one eyebrow rose—along with the smarm factor. "Hello, Starr."

He was slightly taller than Waylon, but that didn't stop Waylon's hands from itching to rearrange the pretty boy's face. Men like him were always more concerned about their looks than the people in their life.

"Ashton." Starr nodded stiffly.

Tension crackled in the air. Waylon wanted to step forward and shield Starr, but that was ridiculous. What was *wrong* with him? This was Noel's kid sister.

She's not a kid anymore.

Therein lay the problem. He hadn't thought of her as anything but. Just because she looked beautiful in a dress and made him smile didn't mean he had to treat her differently.

He blew out a breath and rubbed the back of his neck.

"Hey, Waylon, why don't we head to the living room?" Noel suggested.

Waylon's eyes flicked to Starr and back to Noel. "Sounds like a plan." Hopefully Angel—or Ashton—wouldn't eat Starr alive.

He followed Noel down the hall and into the living room on the right. The space showcased Christmas decorations in their full glory. Right in front of the big picture window stood an artificial green spruce that had been frosted with snow. Silver and blue bulbs covered the tree. A silver star graced the top, glowing among the white lights.

"Nice tree."

"You know my mom." Noel shrugged. "She expects perfection for the holidays."

"Are you sure? Because with Ashton around, you might get less than perfect."

Noel frowned as he sat in the wingback chair across from Waylon. "How's the store?"

"Not today." He let out a groan.

Noel nodded slowly, his expression becoming stern. "Then

maybe we should talk about how you were eyeing my little sister out there."

Heat climbed up Waylon's neck as he floundered for words.

"It was a little disturbing, man. We're talking about my baby sister here."

"I . . ." *What am I supposed to say?*

Noel howled with laughter. "You should see the look on your face." He wiped his eyes.

Waylon rubbed a hand down his pant leg. "I didn't expect her to look so . . . beautiful." *Breathtaking.* Even now, he was waiting for her to join them in the living room so he could be near her again.

Why? He'd *never* reacted to a woman like this before. And it wasn't like he hadn't been around Starr before. Granted, he couldn't remember the last time they'd hung out or if he'd had a girlfriend at the time or not. Maybe that was the problem. He hadn't dated in a couple of years.

"She grew up."

"I noticed." His lips twisted.

Noel shook his head. "Seriously though. She could use a friend. With the whole wedding fiasco, I'm afraid Starr will get lost in the festivities Angel has planned."

"I can't believe Angel and . . ." Waylon blew out a breath.

"Angel's oblivious to others."

Could Waylon hang around Starr and not want anything more than friendship? He thought of her face when she saw Angel and Ashton walk in. Resolve had him nodding. "I can be a friend."

Noel rubbed his chin. "Thank you. You're one of the few friends I'd trust around my sister."

Waylon's leg jostled up and down. *As a friend* were the unspoken words. But at least it gave him an opportunity to ensure Ashton didn't mess with Starr. "Happy to help."

"Thanks, man." Noel sighed. "If she knows she's not alone, maybe the holidays will be enjoyable for her. Angel certainly won't care."

Considering how selfish Angel had always been, Waylon could agree with the assessment. "Consider me Team Starr." He grimaced inwardly. Why was he fumbling for adequate words?

Fortunately, Noel simply nodded.

Waylon sat back, sinking into the pale gray couch cushions. "Is the rest of your family here?"

"Eve's changing, and we're waiting for Dad to return home."

"Working on Thanksgiving?" At Noel's nod, he continued. "How's life at the bank?"

"The same." Noel loosened his tie. "And not. Dad is thinking of retiring."

"Does that mean you're next in line?"

"Most likely."

Waylon let loose a low whistle. "You ready for that responsibility?"

"I've been groomed for it."

"But . . . ?"

Noel shrugged. "Time will tell."

"I'll be praying for you, man."

"Thanks."

Before Noel could continue, Angel and Starr entered the room. He scanned Starr's face, seeking a hint of emotion. Her lips were in a flat line. Did that mean she was irritated? Upset? She sat at the opposite end of the couch he occupied.

"I was telling Starr all the festivities we have planned leading up to the wedding." Angel lowered into a chair, crossing her legs at the same time. She would have been a perfect pageant princess.

"How many are there?" he asked out of curiosity.

26

Angel beamed, flashing her white teeth. Waylon vaguely remembered all the Lewis children in braces at one time or another.

"Well, besides the fittings—"

"What fittings?" Noel interrupted.

"For the groomsmen and bridesmaids."

Noel curled his lip, and Starr stared down at her hands. *Angel wouldn't really . . .*

Waylon inhaled abruptly. "Starr, are you a bridesmaid?" he turned to her.

"Eve and I both are," she said softly.

He bit off a choice word. What was *wrong* with Angel?

"Noel and Gabe will also be groomsmen," Angel said, unaware of the undercurrents filling the air.

"Does Ashton have his friends as groomsmen as well?" Waylon asked.

"Of course." Angel's grin widened. "We have a total of sixteen in the wedding party."

"Sixteen?" *Good grief.* "Including the bride-to-be and groom?"

Angel giggled, covering her mouth and dipping her head. She had to have practiced that in the mirror.

Ashton walked in and stood behind Angel's chair, resting a hand on her shoulder.

"No, silly. Eight bridesmaids and eight groomsmen. Then us." She gasped, looking up and over her shoulder. "Ashton, did you remember to tell your friends about the wedding-favor social?"

Waylon mouthed the words to Noel, who rolled his eyes. Starr rolled her eyes. Waylon leaned to the left, catching Starr's attention. "What's a wedding-favor social?"

"It's when the lucky wedding party gets to put together four hundred party favors for the wedding guests under the guise of food and fun." Starr recited the speech, nailing Angel's pronunciation perfectly.

Waylon's mouth dropped open. "Four hundred?"

"Yes. Want to join in the fun?" She grinned as if anticipating a negative response from him.

"When is it?"

Starr blinked. "Oh no, I didn't really mean . . ." She swallowed. "I mean, you aren't in the wedding party. You don't have to help."

"I want to." And he truly did. He could run interference between Starr and her sister and ex—and get to know her better.

"Really?"

"Really."

"Thank you." She reached out and squeezed his hand.

He enveloped it between his and looked into her eyes. "Anytime."

Her cheeks bloomed with color. He couldn't help but think once more how beautiful she looked.

"Dinner is ready."

Waylon jerked back and smiled at Mrs. Lewis standing in the doorway.

Let the fun begin.

❄ *three* ❄

He just got better looking with age. Waylon's lean facial features fit perfectly with the lanky lines of his body. Yet he possessed an inner strength Starr couldn't help but admire. Or maybe it was his smile that had her mesmerized. When his full lips curved, it transformed his whole face and sent flutters of awareness through her.

He was a much-welcomed distraction from Ashton. She could practically feel her ex staring from all the way across the dinner table. Shouldn't he be focused on Angel?

"So, Waylon, how's the store coming along?" Mom dabbed at her mouth.

Waylon winced. "Still finding my footing."

"I think it's admirable that you're carrying out your mother's wishes."

Starr's eyes flew to Waylon. His mother had passed? When? As if he could hear her mental questions, he met her gaze.

"My mom died six months ago." He took a sip of water. "Now I'm trying to save her store."

"I'm so sorry." Her heart panged in sympathy. As much as her family frustrated her, she couldn't imagine life without a single one of them.

Waylon's expression turned somber. Starr wanted to reach out and offer comfort like he unknowingly had when he agreed to go to Angel's wedding-favor social. She scoffed inwardly. Such a ridiculous notion.

"Maybe Starr could help." Mom beamed at her before turning her attention back to Waylon. "Starr is doing wonderful work at Thomas and Jones PR firm in New York."

Was doing wonderful work, Mom. Apparently, not wonderful enough. Starr's stomach clenched as she struggled to smile at her mom's misplaced pride.

"I'm not surprised." Waylon's steady regard was like a warm hug.

"What do you mean?" she asked.

"I always knew you had a good head on your shoulders. Although, I imagined you as a writer."

Her hand tightened around her fork, her pulse pounding in her ears. Surely he didn't know about the notebook in her luggage that held pages of a fictional story. One she couldn't bring herself to type up on her laptop. Then the attempt would be all too real. Writing in her notebook was a reminder that her love for fiction could only be a hobby. She wasn't talented enough for it to be a full-time reality.

"Oh, Starr writes for her PR firm. Isn't that right, honey?" Mom turned an expectant look on her.

Starr nodded, hoping she didn't resemble a deer in headlights. She shoved a forkful of salad into her mouth. Maybe if she ate more, the questions around her job would stop.

"If you could give me any direction, I'd appreciate it," Waylon said.

"Of course." She didn't need a job to help out a friend.

Waylon's face relaxed into a smile. "Thanks, Starr."

"Enough about Starr." Angel grinned to take the sting from her words.

It didn't work. Starr's stomach roiled as her sister changed the subject to her favorite one—herself.

"Let's talk about the wedding."

"You already sent us an email and a group text and had us download that Discord app." Gabe's mouth turned downward. "Let's enjoy dinner without more wedding talk."

"But, Gabe, the wedding is less than a month away," Angel whined. "I have to make sure everything goes smoothly."

"Isn't that what the wedding planner is for?" Noel asked.

"She's the one who sent out all the communication links. She has temporary access to my email." Angel dabbed primly at her mouth and pushed her food away. "Mom, you made way too much food. I won't be able to fit into my dress if I eat everything."

"Well, honey, you don't have to eat it all. The rest of us are enjoying the meal too. Besides, I had to cook a couple of Starr's favorites."

All heads swung her way. "I appreciate it." Even though not a single one of the dishes was a favorite. Mac and cheese was Gabe's. Angel probably claimed salad was hers, but those meatballs were her true pick. Eve liked sweet potatoes, and Noel was a turkey fanatic. If Starr were to request a dish, then stuffing would be her choice. Only, her mom hated stuffing.

"You're so spoiled," Angel remarked.

Eve snorted. "Says the one demanding attention on Starr's first night back."

"What?" Angel threw her hands up in the air. "Excuse me for wanting my wedding to be perfect."

"Honey, your day will be fabulous." Mom looked at Ashton. "How's your campaign work going?"

"Fantastic. Ms. Martin is leading in the polls and in fundraising. She's sure to win the party vote."

Starr wanted to roll her eyes at his political grin. How had she ever thought him to be sincere and trustworthy?

31

"We'll be sure to vote, won't we?" Her mom attempted to stare at each of them in the eye.

"Supporting Ashton is very important. After all, in a month, he'll be family." Angel looked up at him adoringly.

Starr fought against the rising nausea. Maybe she wouldn't have such a problem with the two of them if they'd bother apologizing for backstabbing her. Instead, they seemed to think she should applaud them for finding their "soul mate."

She took a sip of her drink, cooling the welling rage. It wouldn't do any good to show an emotion other than *happy to be back home*. Her family wouldn't understand the turmoil that made her head ache on a steady basis. How worried she was that not one application she'd filled out would lead to an interview. How she didn't know where she was going to live. How being a failure kept her up at night as she compared her accomplishments—or lack thereof—to her siblings'.

Starr discreetly looked around the table. How long did she have to sit here before she could excuse herself? She was *not* in a festive mood, and if Angel said one more thing about her wedding, Starr would scream.

But you have a month's worth of torture to endure. She bit back a whimper. *Lord, save me now.*

"Don't forget the tree lighting next Thursday." Her father's commanding voice resonated in the dining room.

"But, Dad, that's the day of our wedding-favor social."

He raised an eyebrow. "You won't be stuffing favors all day, Angel."

"It's in the evening."

"Then change it. Tickets are hard to come by."

Her lips pursed.

"Waylon, I have an extra ticket if you'd like to join us." Dad waited expectantly for his answer.

"Thank you, sir. I really appreciate that. I'll be there."

As she watched how comfortable Waylon was around her family, an idea began niggling in the back of her mind. Maybe she should befriend Waylon. Friendship always made the holidays more enjoyable, and this year had to be particularly hard on him since his mom passed. Was his sister around?

Well, she's not at the dinner table, so guess not.

"I expect everyone to be here by six," Dad boomed.

"Yes, sir," they all chorused.

It was like Starr's childhood all over again. Her father never talked much, unless issuing a command he expected to be followed without complaint. Just like when they were kids, Angel had raised an objection before relenting.

Starr peeked at Waylon. What did he think of her family? She remembered how he'd hung around a lot when he and Noel were in high school. But had he come back during college? She wished she could see inside his thoughts . . . or pass a note across the table. Her lips twitched at the thought. He tilted his head as if to ask her what was so funny.

She shook her head slightly, but he discreetly placed his palms together prayer-style and poked out his bottom lip. She snorted, clapping a hand over her mouth and coughing to cover the sound.

"Is there a problem, Starr?" Her father's black eyes locked on to her.

"No, sir. Wrong pipe." She made a show of sipping her drink and sighing loudly afterward. "All better."

"Hmm." Her father checked his watch. "I need to return to the office for a couple of hours."

"Russell!" her mother exclaimed.

"It can't be helped." He kissed her mother on the cheek as he rose. "Happy Thanksgiving, everyone, and welcome home, Starr."

"Thank you, Dad."

He straightened his tie. "Noel?"

"Coming." Noel shoved another bite of food into his mouth, then followed their father out of the dining room.

"May I be excused too?" Starr looked at her mom expectantly.

"Sure, honey. You must be tired from traveling."

More like tired of the forced family cheer. "Like you wouldn't believe."

"Have a nice night, dear."

Starr strode out of the room, thankful to escape and retreat into quiet. She took the stairs until she made it to the attic floor. As she stepped into her room, her mind went back to the past. Her dream board was posted above her old desk, holding pictures of her and her high school friends. Her first car. Her short story that had been printed in the school paper.

"I imagined you as a writer."

Waylon's words echoed in her head. Once upon a time, she'd held that same dream. Yet when she went to college and received advice from her parents, Starr had chosen a communications degree instead of the creative writing one she'd wanted for years.

She shook her head, trying to physically dislodge her thoughts. Heaving her suitcase onto her bed, she unzipped the luggage. She hadn't had time to unpack everything earlier before changing for dinner. Somehow her rummaging through the contents had shifted her notebook to the top, as if waiting for her attention.

The rom-com was an enemies-to-lovers story set in New York. So far, the witty banter between the hero and heroine had her laughing to herself. She slid the notebook onto her desk. Maybe she'd play around with the story in between job hunting.

Or now. You're not doing anything.

She stared at her closed bedroom door. Since the rest of the family was in the dining room, Starr wouldn't have to worry about anyone coming up here. She grabbed a pencil and sat in the white chair in front of the matching desk.

After reading a few sentences to refresh her mind and wake up her creative thinking, Starr started writing once more.

"Do you need a bib, baby?"

"Did you just call me 'baby'?" Aria's eyes flashed with fire.

"Not in a romantic sense. You've got a stain a mile wide on your shirt."

She froze, horror dropping her jaw. Slowly she looked down to see that guacamole had dropped from her tortilla chip and made a slimy trail down her beautiful white sweater. Was it possible to die from mortification?

Starr looked down at the words she'd written. They were trash. This was why writing would only be a hobby for her. She didn't have what it took to make it into a career. She used her eraser and got rid of the new words, hating that her insides felt like curling into a fetal position. But if she didn't like her own writing, surely no one else would.

She closed the notebook and rose. Going back to her suit-case, Starr peeked at all the clothes she'd stuffed inside. Since she wasn't going anywhere anytime soon, it would be a good time to hang up things in her old closet. Hopefully she had packed enough clothes to get her through the holidays and on to the next job.

"Welcome back, Starr," she murmured.

❄ *four* ❄

Waylon leaned against the wall as some of the Lewis family filtered out of the home to go to the National Christmas Tree Lighting Ceremony.

"Let's go, Starr," Noel called. "We're going to be late."

"Sorry, Noel." She stepped down the last step and hustled down the hallway. "Misplaced my phone."

Her pale blue peacoat came to her knees and a white-and-blue scarf filled the open collar of her jacket. She looked beautiful. And surely not the reason he hung around with Noel instead of going with the others.

Be her friend, not a creeper. He shifted on his feet.

"Did you find it?" Noel slid his hands into gloves.

"I did." She came to a halt, noticing Waylon for the first time. "Hey, Waylon." Her lips curved into a smile.

"Hey." He groaned inwardly. *That's it?*

Starr turned to her brother. "Are we driving?"

"No. Dad suggested we take the Metro. The streets closer to the White House are closed for the tree lighting."

"Makes sense."

"Everyone else literally just walked out." Noel pointed out the door. "So we can still catch up."

"Did you volunteer to wait for me?" Starr asked.

"Of course. Waylon too." Noel held the front door open.

Waylon begged his cheeks not to flush or show how the nonchalant comment from Noel affected him. Well, rather, what Starr thought about Noel's comment.

They headed down the street to the Metro stop. Waylon pulled his beanie farther down on his head as he followed Noel. He glanced at Starr, noting her short legs trying to keep up. "Slow down, man."

"Thanks." She shot him a grateful look.

"If you were back in New York, what would you be doing?" He slid his hands into his coat pockets.

"Well, I've been to the lighting ceremony at Rockefeller Center. But most likely, I'd be working." Sadness darkened her eyes.

Why did that make her sad? He went with a neutral question instead. "What did you do all day?"

"Relaxed. You guys?" She motioned between Noel and Waylon.

For a moment, Waylon had forgotten Noel was with them.

"I was knee-deep in paperwork at the bank." Noel shot her a look as if to say *What else would I be doing?*

Starr shook her head. "Of course you were. What about you, Waylon?"

"I stocked shelves in between customers."

"Oh, I should check out the store." She clasped her gloved hands together. "Are you open on the weekends?"

"Just Saturday." His mom had never worked on Sundays, choosing to observe a day of rest.

He bit back the sigh at the thought of her. All around the shop were memories of her, and now he was making new holiday memories without her. It didn't seem right, but sitting in his place all alone didn't make it any better.

They slowed as the bus stop came into view. The rest of the Lewis family still waited by the sign. Noel walked faster and went to stand by his father, so Waylon took a step closer to Starr.

"Whenever you choose to come, I'll give you the grand tour."

"Thanks." She tucked her chin, then peered up at him through veiled lashes. "Have you been to the tree lighting before?"

"Never." Excitement had added a little pep to his step when he'd closed up shop.

"You'll love it. We'll have to make sure it's memorable for you." She buried her chin, as if the thirty-degree weather was unbearable for her.

He wanted to cheer her up. "How 'bout we start with a selfie?" He pulled his cell phone out of his coat pocket.

Her head jerked up. "Yes!"

Why did her enthusiasm unlock something within him? He lowered his head next to hers. She smelled like Christmas—all cinnamon and sugar—and the urge to nuzzle his nose to her neck overwhelmed him. His face heated at the thought, but he focused on smiling like this was just a friendly picture.

"Say Christmas lights!"

Starr chuckled. "Christmas lights!"

Waylon snapped a few photos and then straightened. He showed her his favorite.

"You can't even see a height difference." Her gaze roamed from his feet to his face. "How tall are you?"

"Six feet." His lips quirked. "What are you? Five feet?"

"And one inch," she added smartly.

He bit back a chuckle. "Oh, five-one. My mistake."

"Hey." She nudged him. "That extra inch is very important."

"I'm sure. Probably gets you on all the rides, huh?"

"Ha." Her lips twitched, showing she took the joke in stride. "What about you? Six feet even isn't impressive."

"Sure it is. Don't you know the taller you are, the smarter you are?"

Her mouth gaped. "What?"

Waylon shook his head. "Sorry, that sounded a lot funnier in my head." He rubbed the back of his neck. "I'm actually a little mortified. Hopefully apologizing isn't difficult with my big foot stuck in my mouth. Forgive me?"

She studied him a moment. "As long as you admit I'm smarter, all is forgiven."

"Oh, you're definitely smarter." Cute too. Why did Noel's little sister have to be so captivating?

"I know." She winked, then followed her family onto the bus.

Waylon sat next to Starr, and she told him about New York and what the city looked like decorated for Christmas.

"Is it colder up there?"

"Nope. It was in the fifties when I left."

He sighed. "That sounds nice right about now. Think we'll freeze when we get to the White House?"

"Definitely." She grinned. "Will you wimp out?"

A bark of laughter flew from his lips. Noel turned around, raising an eyebrow. Waylon gulped. Was that a *Stay away from my sister* look or *What's so funny*?

He looked down into her pretty eyes. "I won't wimp out."

"Neither will I. But if you do wimp out, you owe me a hot chocolate."

"Deal."

They continued talking until they filed off the bus and walked toward the White House. After going through security procedures, Waylon found himself on the lawn in front of the

National Christmas Tree. His head inclined back as his gaze swept the full height to view all the ornaments on the way to the top, where a single star stood.

"It's beautiful," Starr said.

"Agreed."

"Hey, you two," Noel said, coming up to them. "Dad wants to get seated."

Waylon motioned for Starr to walk in front of him. He placed a hand against her back, making sure no one else bumped into her. Soon they were seated with the rest of the people.

Then the president and first lady walked onto the stage. Waylon couldn't help but feel a little awestruck.

He leaned down to whisper in Starr's ear. "This is amazing."

She nodded, eyes focused forward.

He tuned in as the crowd around them began counting down. "Three . . . two . . . one . . ."

Silence filled the air for a long moment, then it was swallowed by the crowd's applause as the tree lit up. Waylon whistled with a few other citizens. This truly was a majestic sight. How many lights were strung together to make the blue spruce stand out like that? How many ornaments had they used?

His mom would have loved to see something like this. Maybe even wished for the opportunity to make an ornament or two. His smile slipped as the realization that she wasn't here to enjoy this punched him in the gut once more.

A tug on his arm caught his attention. Starr motioned for him to lean closer.

"Don't forget to take a pic."

"Right." He snapped a few horizontal ones, then rotated his

phone for a vertical view. "Hey, take one with me, and I'll get the tree in the background."

Starr's dad had gotten them seats up close. Waylon should easily be able to get the tree in the background. He bent his knees in order to place his face near Starr's to take a few more photos. He took his time, reveling at her nearness. He snapped a final frame, then stood to his full height.

The first family walked off stage, and a country music duo took their place. They got the crowd clapping as they sang a twangy rendition of "Rudolph the Red-Nosed Reindeer." After them, another artist took the stage. The music continued, showcasing different artists from a variety of genres, as they serenaded the crowd. When a famous R&B singer took the stage, Starr whispered in Waylon's ear, sending shivers down his neck.

"Everyone's getting ready to head out. Dad doesn't want to be caught up in the crowd, and he has it on good authority that this is the last song."

"Lead the way."

Starr smiled and followed her siblings out of the row and down the aisle. Some people seated in the back were already moving toward the exit. Waylon checked his cell for the time. *Nine o'clock.* Not too late. Maybe they could stop for an evening snack.

You just want to spend more time with Starr.

True. Something about her made his life seem brighter and full of hope. The grief wasn't so prominent with her around. Not that that was the only reason he wanted to know more about her. But maybe keeping in mind that grief was still very present in his life should keep him from crossing any lines.

As they turned onto the sidewalk, the family members began pairing off. Mr. and Mrs. Lewis led the way with Noel and Eve behind them, then Angel and Ashton, leaving Gabe to form a trio with Waylon and Starr at the rear.

"I'm starving," Gabe remarked.

"I was thinking about getting something to eat too." Waylon looked at Starr. "What do you think?"

"That sounds good."

Angel turned around. "Are you guys going somewhere to eat?"

"You know we are, Angel." Gabe smirked at his twin.

"Where are we going?" she asked.

Waylon wanted to object because where Angel went, Ashton slinked behind her.

"Grilled Cheese Bar?" Gabe suggested.

Waylon shook his head. "They're closed by now."

"Old Ebbit Grill?" Angel asked.

"Sounds good," Gabe said.

"What do you think, Starr?" Waylon didn't want her to feel pressured to go now that Angel and Ashton had invited themselves. Yet he wanted to spend time with her—and not only because Noel suggested it.

"Sure." But her smile looked a little forced, and her voice didn't hold the same excitement as earlier.

Waylon wanted to shoo the Double A's away. Didn't they care how Starr felt about their presence? Then again, Angel did make Starr a bridesmaid, so that showed how her sister rated on the care-factor scale.

He exhaled and moved closer to Starr. "You can sit by me and continue telling me all about New York."

"Or maybe you can tell me about your store." The lights glittered in her eyes as she smiled up at him.

Was that his heart thumping, or did he have indigestion? There was something about Starr Lewis that struck him, making him more introspective than normal. Even though it had been a couple of years since he'd dated, other women had caught his eye. Yet she was the first who made him want to know her more.

They walked up Fifteenth Street and entered Old Ebbit Grill. Tantalizing smells greeted them, and Waylon's stomach responded as if only just realizing it was famished. Noel and Eve had declined the late-night dinner invitation and had followed their parents home.

As the rest of them sat at a table, Waylon discreetly examined Ashton. Angel's fiancé had a slick demeanor to him that made it easy for Waylon to imagine him schmoozing Washington's elite. He could understand Angel falling for that kind of guy, but Starr . . .

What had she seen in him? And did Waylon have any chance of being more than just friends with her?

Slow your roll, dude. Noel asked you to be a friend. Plus, she's only here for the holidays. Do you really want to start a relationship that will be long distance and most likely break your heart?

He reached for his glass of water. *Probably not.*

"I haven't been here in forever." Angel flipped her hair over her shoulder. "What are you guys going to get?" She winked at Gabe. "Of course, everyone knows you're getting wings."

The rest of them laughed.

"Hey, you can't ruin wings." Gabe threw his balled-up straw wrapper at Angel.

"Take a risk and try something different. Maybe the oysters?"

Gabe made a face reminiscent of a toddler eating vegetable baby food for the first time.

Starr closed her menu. "I'm getting the clam chowder."

Waylon smiled as she blew on her hands to warm them. "Are you cold?"

"A bit."

"You're always cold." Ashton smirked.

Both Angel and Starr froze. Waylon could feel the tension pouring off Starr, and Angel's smile looked like it would crack any second.

A server came, interrupting the moment with a request for drink orders. Waylon watched Ashton out of the corner of his eye. He wasn't so naïve as to think no other man had dated two sisters, but the smugness that clung to Ashton left a bad taste in Waylon's mouth. There was no remorse in Ashton's expressions, just an oily residue.

"Did you reschedule the wedding-favor social?" Gabe asked, either ignoring the tension in the air or trying to break it.

Starr let out a breath.

Angel nodded. "I did. It looks like Wednesday evening will be the best time for all in the wedding party."

"Not for me." Gabe frowned. "Dad expects me to stay late at the bank that day."

"I told him I need you more."

"Did he agree to that?"

"Of course." Angel shrugged one shoulder.

Did she always get her way? Waylon remembered Angel being vain as a child, but had she always been this self-centered?

"Fine. I'll be there."

"Since you aren't doing anything, Starr, you can help me take the items over to Ashton's parents' place."

"All right."

Starr's voice had gotten quiet. Waylon couldn't sit by and let her get railroaded by her obnoxious sister. Not to mention the thought of having the party at Ashton's didn't sit too well with him.

"I was planning on giving Starr a ride over. Can she come

the same time as everyone else?" He purposely contorted his features into a sheepish expression. "I doubt I could close the store earlier."

Something like irritation flashed across Angel's face. But the small hand that found his under the table and gave it a squeeze made Angel's annoyance fall like water down his back.

"That's fine." Ashton looked at Angel. "My friends can help you. Remember, they're on vacation just like Starr."

"But she's my sister," Angel pouted.

"I'm helping Waylon," Starr said. "His store needs some marketing help."

"Oh. Well, in that case, come with everyone else."

Angel turned toward Ashton, and the two commenced whispering, their heads close together.

"Who thinks they're talking about us?" Gabe asked in a low voice.

"Most likely me," Starr replied.

"Nah." Waylon shook his head. "Definitely me, since I stole you away from their clutches."

Starr chuckled, schooling her face into an expression of perfect calm as Angel whipped her head in Starr's direction.

"See?" she mumbled.

"I think you're right. Guess now you'll really have to help me out Wednesday." Waylon took another sip of his drink.

"I can come in Monday too." She turned to look at him. "I'd like to shadow you Monday and possibly Tuesday. Then Wednesday we can sit down and talk about what I noticed and what your vision is."

"I'd really appreciate that." He didn't want to fail the store or his mom's trust in him.

"Think of it as payback for teaching me how to ride a bike."

Wow. "How do you even remember that? I'd totally forgotten." He grinned at the memory, picturing Starr with two pigtails and a death grip on her bike.

Starr had come into Noel's room in tears because no one would teach her how to ride her bike, and she didn't want to enter the fourth grade riding a bike with training wheels. Noel had immediately taken her out to their driveway to teach her, but he'd barked out orders like a drill sergeant, adding to her misery. Waylon had taken him aside and offered to teach her, same as he'd taught his own sister. After a half hour, Starr had been riding with ease.

"I haven't. You've always had a kindness about you." She nudged him with her elbow. "Do you still have those chivalry skills?"

"For you, I'll dust them off and put them to use." Was that too cheesy?

Her cheeks darkened, and her lashes fluttered as if trying to hide the expression behind them.

Maybe not. He lowered his voice. "Did I embarrass you or just myself?"

Starr shook her head. "You have nothing to be embarrassed about." She straightened in her seat and turned to Gabe.

Had he just been dismissed? Dismay speared him. Why had he flirted with her? Hadn't Noel warned him that she needed a friend? Waylon could kick himself for adding to Starr's awkwardness of sitting across from her ex-boyfriend by having her brother's best friend flirting with her when she had no interest in him.

Though the thought hurt more than he wanted to admit, he felt more shame at ruining the lighthearted mood she'd managed to have despite the knuckleheads sitting across from them. Waylon tried not to let the thoughts weigh him down, but he couldn't stop his mind from thinking and asking question after question.

Lord, please guide me and grant me wisdom. I want to know Starr better. And I want her to want the same thing as well.

Because claiming he was trying to only be a friend would be a lie. But if that's what she needed, he would swallow his pride and set the flirting to zero.

❄ *five* ❄

Starr flipped down the visor and gave one last glance to her hair and makeup. She repositioned some of her curls in the front and touched up her lip gloss.

Why are you primping?

This was Waylon—her brother's best friend and the guy who taught her to ride a bike. Just thinking it was enough to make her face scrunch up. Why did she have to remind Waylon of her as a crying child? When he'd flirted with her—*Lord, please let that be his intentions*—she'd panicked. She didn't have it all together like Eve, and she certainly wasn't polished like Angel. Feelings of inadequacy had coursed through her, and embarrassment had her distancing herself.

Only, Starr couldn't help but want to hang around Waylon. He made her laugh and feel calmer around her chaotic family. Not to mention the sparks that appeared when he turned that charming grin her way. Could he actually see her as more than Noel's baby sister?

Only one way to find out.

She stared at the sidewalk leading to his shop. "You can do this, Starr. Treat this visit like the business it is, and if anything else happens . . ." Then she'd go from there.

Exiting her car, she joined the other shoppers heading down the sidewalk in the streets of Alexandria, Virginia. A walk down the block landed her in front of Forever Christmas. She took in the redbrick storefront that sat on the corner of Main Avenue. The sign was a little outdated above the black door, and the window display somewhat lackluster. Nothing about the view made her want to come inside and look around.

Starr took out her cell and quickly jotted the observation down in her notes app before entering the shop. Christmas music greeted her, bringing a smile to her face, and the scent of pine made her think of Christmas morning. The atmosphere in the shop definitely put a customer in the Christmas mood. *A plus for Waylon.*

As she studied the store, Starr continued taking notes. Like the fact that no one had greeted her, making the store seem unattended. Next came the observation that the shelves hadn't experienced a good dusting in a while. If he kept it up, he'd have his own faux snow. She squinted at a nearby display. *Never mind, that is snow.* Surely there was a better product to provide a winter look versus one that would have patrons whipping out hand sanitizer.

Not only that, but none of the displays were cohesive. The lack of organization could overwhelm customers who liked to see all ornaments in one section and Christmas stockings in another. Had the shop been like this when Waylon's mom had run it? She bit her lip. Starr would have to moderate her words when offering suggestions. No way she wanted to insult Waylon's mom or the memories that surely existed in the place.

Waylon walked through a doorway and paused, box in hand, before his full lips curved. "Hey there. When did you get here?" He placed the carboard container on the checkout counter.

"About five minutes ago." She smiled, her heart fluttering as she stepped closer.

"I'm sorry. My front doorbell must be broken." He walked over, opened the door, and frowned. "Yep." He ran a hand over the top of his small 'fro. "One more thing to add to my list."

"Hey." Starr laid a hand on his forearm. "I'll help. That's why I'm here."

"Thank you. I can't tell you how much I appreciate you. I figured you'd just tell me to get a website and then bounce."

Her mouth dropped open. "You don't have a website?"

A sheepish grin covered his face as he shook his head.

"Social media sites?"

He shook it once more.

Oh no. "Email?"

Waylon chuckled. "I do have a store email and business cards. Mom liked the personal touch."

"You need a website stat, along with a social media presence. An online presence will get customers into your store. And if you're willing to mail items, you can reach customers around the world."

"Add that to the list."

She held up her cell. "Already started one."

"Really?" His eyes widened.

Was he worried? She nodded.

Waylon groaned, sliding his hands into his pockets. "All right. Do you want to give me a first impression?"

"Are you ready for it?" Maybe this wasn't such a good idea. She was interested in Waylon, and telling him his store needed an upgrade might keep her in the friend zone—or best friend's little sister zone, if there was such a thing.

"Not really. When I first started working here, I had so many ideas on how to transform the business. It was more to help her out, not with the idea I would ever run the business.

I'd just graduated with a master's, so I was feeling myself out a bit." He smirked. "Unfortunately, Mom didn't like any of my suggestions and thought I needed more retail experience."

Starr could understand that. "Did you get a degree in marketing?"

Amusement twinkled in his russet-colored eyes. "I barely passed my marketing courses. Not my strong suit. My undergrad was a basic business degree, and my master's was in nonprofit management."

"Why nonprofit?"

His face flushed. "I really like working with youth. In fact, I was working at a community center when my mom passed. Once her will was read, giving us ownership of the shop, I had a conversation with my sister, and we both agreed I'd take over running the place."

"I'm so sorry for your loss." She paused, searching for the appropriate words and tone. "Are you ready to maintain ownership? Waylon, do you *want* to keep the store?"

His cheeks puffed with air. The sigh hadn't been audible, but fatigue and worry were written all over his face.

"I'm not sure. I want to honor Mom and the legacy she built here. But I never imagined owning a Christmas shop."

"What was your plan?"

"Starting a nonprofit to help youth, specifically minority kids who don't have the same opportunities as other more advantaged teens."

That was admirable. Waylon had a kindness about him that struck her right in the heart. She could only imagine how kids would respond to his humor and easy manner. If she threw her arms around him and begged him to take her out, how desperate would that register her on the scale?

Remember, you don't live here full-time.

But just one date.

Starr blinked, trying to wipe away her thoughts. "That's a great idea. Right now, how about I continue shadowing you? I'll write up some marketing suggestions, and then when the store closes, share everything with you. After that, the ball will be in your court."

"Sounds like I have a lot of praying to do. Thanks, Starr."

"Sure thing." She bit her lip. "I'll pray for you too."

"I appreciate that."

Before he could say anything further, the door opened, and a customer walked in. Starr moved to the side and watched the exchange.

The next hour passed quietly with only a few customers coming in. After the last customer left, Waylon took her to the back, where boxes of inventory were stored. He opened one and lifted a handmade ornament from the box.

"I can't believe someone made this." She held up the blown-glass ornament. "How did you even find the artist?"

"Mom did." Waylon got a faraway look in his eyes. "She ran into a woman at the post office who needed help with boxes. Mom helped her carry a bunch in, and they got to talking. Next thing I know, Mom came in with a box of ornaments, and we've done business together ever since. The artist even came to the funeral."

"Your mom was always so kind to me, I shouldn't be surprised." She looked up at Waylon. "And you inherited that trait."

"Nah. I'm only nice when I like someone." His jaw clamped shut, and he rubbed his chin. "Uh, I didn't mean to make you uncomfortable."

"Did I say I was?" Had she been giving him a *back off* vibe without realizing it?

"Really?" He studied her, as if testing the truth of her statement.

"Truly."

Waylon stepped closer, his eyes dropping to her lips. Her breath hitched while her stomach dipped with want. When had anyone ever looked at her with such longing and desire?

She stretched up on her toes and leaned forward as Waylon cupped her elbows to hold her steady.

"Waylon, yoo-hoo!" a voice called.

He jerked back, his attention shifting toward the front. Starr came back down to solid ground, head out of the clouds and disappointment pulling her lips downward.

"Uh, I need to see who that is. I think it's Mrs. Hayes."

"Should I continue unboxing the inventory?"

"No. I'll get it." He held up a finger. "Be right back."

She blew out a breath as he retreated. *What just happened?* She placed her palms to her cheeks.

More accurately, what hadn't?

Waylon had been so close to kissing her, which thrilled and terrified her all in one breath. She wanted to see where this would go, but her life was a mess. Could she actually pursue a relationship with Waylon, knowing she wanted to find a new job back in the city? She wasn't a holiday-fling kind of girl and couldn't imagine Waylon was the type not to want commitment. What would he say to all the thoughts and questions gathering speed in her mind?

She groaned, flopping into his desk chair. The lines between business and pleasure had been all but erased. Yet nothing had happened. If she ignored it, maybe he would too. All she had to do was focus on his business. Since he wouldn't let her help with inventory, she could start building him a website.

Back in New York, Starr had helped a few of her friends with their websites. Nowadays, there were so many hosts offering free websites, one could be built in a matter of minutes.

She could create a mock-up, and if Waylon didn't like the design, no harm done.

The minutes flew by as she set up the website on the laptop she'd pulled from her purse. Thank goodness for miniature ones that traveled so well. She created a quick logo with a Christmas tree in the back and glass ornaments hanging from it.

She gasped.

That's it!

Waylon could set up a few Christmas trees in the store. If he purchased artificial ones, then they could be up all year round. Decorating each one with a different theme would give inspiration to the customers and make him stand out against any competitors. Since they were already in the holiday season, all the best Christmas ornaments needed to be out, front and center. When the other holidays rolled around, he could change the themed ornaments to fit that particular holiday.

Starr rubbed her hands in glee, which was how Waylon found her when he walked back into his office.

"Uh-oh. You look like you're up to no good."

She laughed and quickly told him her plan for the ornament displays.

"I like it." He leaned against the doorframe.

"Great. When can we go shopping?"

He glanced at his watch. "The shop closes at six. Do you want to grab dinner and then go get the trees?"

Her heart tripped in her chest. Having dinner alone with Waylon sounded like a date. Dare she clarify?

"Um, should I invite Gabe or Noel to join us? Then we could ask them to help decorate too." She watched Waylon for a reaction.

"Okay," he replied slowly. "That could work."

Then they were going to ignore the near kiss. Good. *It's bet-*

ter this way. She forced her lips upward. "Okay. Let me text them and see if they can come."

Please let them say yes, Lord. I can't dine with Waylon by myself. I can't enter a relationship even if I really want to. I need to get my life together first. She was so tired of coming up short. Not to mention that if she got another job back in New York, she wouldn't be in DC much longer.

> **Starr**
> Can you help decorate some trees tonight for Waylon's shop? If so, we'll have dinner at 6 p.m. first.

She sent the text to both of her brothers and waited for a notification to ping.

> **Noel**
> I wish, but we have a business dinner at seven.

> **Gabe**
> I don't even know why I have to go along. We all know Noel's next in line.

> **Noel**
> Quit your whining.

Brothers. Sibling rivalry ran rampant in her family, but it released some of her own anxiety. It was good to know she wasn't the only one who battled with feelings of inadequacy. Still, she *was* the only Lewis sibling unemployed.

"They can't make it." She glanced up at Waylon, who quickly made his face look neutral, but not before an expression of relief had passed. Did he want to be alone with her? *Oh no, I'm going to have to explain why now's a bad time for a relationship, aren't I?*

"Are you still able to help, or do you have to do something with the family as well?"

She met Waylon's gaze, trying not to melt within the depths of his beautiful eyes. "I'd love to spend time with you." Heat flared through her. "I mean, help you decorate." *See, this is why I can't trust myself right now.*

"Right. I thought that's what you meant." His face was completely blank.

Which made her blunder even more embarrassing. Maybe that almost-kiss had all been her imagination.

"Besides, when I ask you on a date, you'll know."

Her stomach dropped to her toes. So not her imagination at all. *Lord, help!*

❄ six ❄

How do you suppose we'll fit all of these trees in the car?" Waylon's eyebrows rose.

He'd been impressed with Starr's idea of having themed trees. Only they'd both forgotten about space—or the lack thereof—in his Nissan Versa.

"Obviously, you'll put the backseats down." She tilted her head. "Angle the biggest box to fit."

"And the other two?"

"Stack the middle one on top or beside the big one. The little one can fit up front with me."

He stared at the rear hatchback, imagining the boxes like Tetris blocks. "Won't that be a little uncomfortable for you?"

She shrugged. "I'll live."

"All right." He popped the trunk and lowered the backseats. After shoving the box forward and tilting it to the left, Waylon smiled. "Okay, this might work after all."

"See?" Starr grabbed the smallest tree. "I'll put this up front."

He nodded, lifting the second box on top of the first. It went in without protest. Maybe his car wasn't as small as he thought. He closed the trunk and walked around to the driver's side.

"Back to the store?" He turned to Starr. *Lord, why did You make her so pretty?*

"Yes. I know it's a little late for work, but people will notice the trees right away when they walk in tomorrow morning."

"Thanks, Starr." He reached over the console and squeezed her hand.

The hairs on his arms rose at the contact. It was like his nerve endings were aware of something momentous happening. The skin contact should have been a simple touch, but reality said it was so much more. He slowly withdrew his hand, faking steadiness and praying she didn't see the slight tremble in his fingers.

"You're welcome." She smiled.

Being around Starr made him want a relationship with her even more. Only, he still wasn't sure she was over Ashton. There was so much potential baggage that his logical side kept pointing out. Angel marrying her ex meant Ashton would always be in their lives. Not to mention his own baggage. He was grieving his mother and ran a business that was struggling to stay in the black. His brain kept warning him to ignore the feelings being around her brought up.

But his heart . . . his heart was already entangled. It didn't help that his emotions were applauding the whole potential scenario of them as a couple.

Quiet descended between them as Waylon drove back to the shop. Hopefully by the time they arrived, he'd figure out how to loosen his tongue and strike up intelligent conversation, but for now, his brain replayed the feel of her hand in his.

"What do you have planned for tomorrow?" Starr's voice broke his introspection.

"Just the normal workday. You? Going to do anything fun?"

She hummed softly. "I think I'll come back and help you with the store again."

"You sure you wouldn't want to do anything more exciting?" He glanced at her, then back to the road.

"Well, I do have a dress fitting at two."

"Are you looking forward to it?" He still couldn't believe that Angel would ask that of her.

"Meh."

He bit back a chuckle. "Not into that type of thing?"

"I love dressing up. Always have. But my idea of fun doesn't involve being a bridesmaid to someone who doesn't want me to be in her wedding."

"What?" Shock coursed through him. "Surely Angel wants you there. Eve's in the bridal party too, right?" Angel was self-centered, but he'd never say she didn't love her family.

"We're in the wedding because we're her sisters, not because she wants us to be. A little birdie told me my mom made her."

So maybe Angel had a heart after all and didn't want to subject Starr to the nuptials? But why would her mom want that? "Who was the birdie? Noel?"

"Angel."

Waylon blinked, sure he'd misheard. "Your sister told you she was forced to make you a bridesmaid?"

"Yep. Called me spoiled, since I'm the 'baby' of the family." Notes of derision filled her voice.

Waylon's heart ached. Starr sure had been through a lot. "Are you upset?" he asked softly.

"About what?"

"How about you start with if you are, then tell me why."

"Okay," she murmured. "I'm upset that my sister stole my boyfriend without a backward glance. She didn't care that we were dating. She thinks that since Ashton broke up with me before they officially got together, I shouldn't have a problem with their relationship."

Waylon tried to wrap his mind around the details. "So wait. Did he cheat on you?"

"We were dating when Angel came to visit me. Ashton took one look at her and dumped me later that evening with the intention of asking her out." She paused. "Does that sound like him cheating on me?"

"Was there some kind of waiting period?" His hands clenched the steering wheel. He'd have to pray not to rearrange Ashton's smarmy face the next time he saw him.

"None. He left my apartment and went straight to the hotel Angel was staying at." Her voice cracked at the end.

Waylon held out his hand, palm up, hoping to offer comfort. She slid her hand against his, and he squeezed her fingers.

"I'm assuming Angel didn't turn him down?" He peeked at Starr.

She shook her head. "It's not like we're best friends or super close as sisters. She's always treated me as a last-minute replacement for whoever she actually wanted to hang out with. Her time in New York was no different. Her other friend ended up sick, so Angel dragged me all over the city for a shopping excursion."

"Has your relationship always been like that?"

"Where Angel thinks the world revolves around her?"

He chuckled wryly. "Yes."

"Yep."

"And your parents never say anything?" Waylon began moving his thumb across the back of her hand. Should he continue holding her hand or let go?

"No. They're quite happy orbiting her."

He laughed at the image that painted.

Waylon parked behind the building and turned to Starr. "I'd happily orbit you." Horror flooded his insides. Not only was that incredibly cheesy, but way to throw his heart at her feet. *Not cool! Weren't you supposed to maintain distance?*

Starr's face flushed, and she dipped her chin. "Waylon . . ."

He sighed. "I understand."

"No. It's just . . ." She looked up to meet his gaze. "I'm here on vacation." Her tongue darted across her lips.

Waylon had to command his brain to return his gaze to her eyes and prevent the image of her lips from looping in his brain.

"Starting something wouldn't be fair to either one of us," Starr continued.

"I get that. . . ." He'd told himself those same things. Yet something about her made him want to take the risk.

"But?" She arched an eyebrow.

"How often do you feel sparks with another person?"

She bit her lip. "Please don't make this any more difficult."

"Why not?" He cupped her cheek. "I want to see where this goes, even if it means I end up communicating long distance and missing you something fierce."

"Waylon . . ." she whispered.

"Say yes." Peace flooded him. This was the right choice. No hiding behind grief, long distance, or any other excuses they could come up with. "Give me a chance. Give *us* a chance."

"I . . ."

"The word you're looking for starts with a *y*."

She shoved his arm as a tinkle of laughter filled the interior of the car. Starr looked so happy he couldn't help himself. His lips were on hers before he could recognize the move, but at her hesitant response, he broke off.

"I'm so sorry." Heat flooded his neck. "I should have asked permission."

"No. There's no need." She circled her arms around his neck and pressed her mouth firmly against his.

Heat poured through him, but he kept the kiss light, wanting to make sure she was okay with it. A soft sigh slipped from her mouth, and he pulled back some, caressing her lower lip with his own. Her lids fluttered open, and something that resembled surprise filled her eyes.

"Penny for your thoughts?" His voice sounded calm, but the husky tone gave away his emotions. No surprise considering that kiss rocked him down to his core.

A smile teased at the corner of her mouth. "You kissed them all away."

His grin let loose, unbidden by her words. He'd known the attraction was mutual. At least, he'd been mostly sure. *Thanks, Lord, for not making this turn disastrous.*

"So now would be a good time to send my subliminal messages through, huh?"

Amusement made her eyes twinkle. "What messages?"

"Go on a date with me." He kissed her right cheek. "Like me." He pressed his lips to her left cheek. "Give me a chance." A kiss to the forehead. "Give us a chance." He brushed her lips once more, then scooted backward, breaking contact. "Don't answer now. Tell me tomorrow."

Her shoulders rose. "Okay."

"Good." He didn't want to rush her response, merely wanted to give Starr reasons to truly consider dating him as an option. "Let's go put these trees up."

They brought everything inside, and Starr gave orders of where she wanted everything set up. She set the small tree on the checkout counter, then turned to him.

"I think you should decorate this one with the glass ornaments. That way you don't have to worry about any kiddos knocking them off. You'll want your sturdier ornaments on the other two."

"Makes sense. How about you decorate the baby one."

"Oh, believe me, I was planning on it." She did a shimmy.

He shook with suppressed laughter. "Before you start, tell me what to do with the big tree."

She came around the corner and walked toward the display window. "Put it right in front of here. That way, whatever seasonal ornaments you're selling will catch the eye of pedestrians. If you have knickknacks that could be set on the ledge, even better."

"There's a nativity scene that could work on the windowsill." He grabbed the tree around the middle and moved it near the window.

"That sounds perfect."

"Good."

She snapped her fingers. "Oh, snap." She giggled.

Had his kisses put her in such a good mood? His chest puffed a little. "What's up?"

"I knew I was forgetting something. I wanted to buy you better snow. This other stuff makes the shop look dusty."

He grimaced. "Agreed. It was another thing my mom preferred."

"Are you good with something different?"

"Definitely."

"Then I'll buy some on the way over tomorrow."

"Thanks. I'll reimburse you."

"You don't have to. It can be my Christmas present to you."

He shook his head. "No offense, but fake snow is a terrible Christmas gift."

Starr doubled over with laughter.

"Why is that so funny?"

"I just pictured you opening a gift and seeing that." She shook her head, still amused. "And the utter disappointment. You're right. That's a terrible gift."

"Then we're in agreement. Will you let me reimburse you?"

"No." She smirked. "But I will get you a better present."

"Thank goodness."

"So speaking of things to change . . ."

He hung some ornaments on the tree. "I don't think we were actually talking about changing things. My mind remembers presents."

"Oh, but we—" She pinned him with a narrowed gaze. "You're joking with me."

"It's easy to."

Starr's lips puckered in a wry grin. "As I was about to say, you need to change the shop name."

His heart clenched. Making small changes here and there to help the business wasn't so bad. But the name? It was almost like erasing his mother. "You don't like Forever Christmas?"

She bit her lip and slowly shook her head.

He sighed. He wasn't a huge fan either, but it seemed disloyal to admit it. *Don't you want to make the store better?* "What do you have in mind?"

"How about Things Yule Love?" Starr eyed him expectantly.

"Like a Yuletide log?"

"Exactly." She beamed at him.

"Funny but no." It was as bad as any dad joke.

"Yule Be Back?"

"No! Enough with the Yule jokes, please."

Starr laughed. "Okay. How about Claus's Closet?"

"Now I'm thinking of Plato's Closet."

She tapped her fingers together. "The Christmas Shoppe?"

"Won't people expect more than ornaments at a store with that name?"

She nodded. "You're probably right. What about 'Tis the Season?"

"To be jolly? No thanks."

"Humbug."

Well, he was beginning to feel Scrooge-like with these names too. He just needed to come up with a better one. "I got it. How about The Christmas Stocking?"

"But you don't sell just stockings."

This was harder than he realized. "Elves at Work?"

"Meh."

"Hold that thought." He held up a finger. "I'm going to grab the nativity display."

"I'll be here."

He went right to the back shelf that held his mom's favorite nativity scene. It was the first one she owned and one she liked to pull out and discuss nostalgic memories over. But when her business had picked up some years back, she'd bought a bigger nativity scene, choosing to keep this one in her office. Every fond memory Waylon held was attached to this particular set, so it was the one *he* wanted out on the window ledge.

I'm doing all of this for you, Mom. I hope you'd be proud. He sighed and headed back to the front.

As soon as he walked through the doorway, Starr offered another name suggestion. "Joyful Memories?"

"Better, but I'm not sure it immediately translates to Christmas."

A pensive look covered her face. "Christmas Treasures?"

"Sounds like a kids' fundraiser."

"Maybe a little," she grudgingly agreed.

She looked so cute disgruntled. He placed the pieces of the set in the window display. "What about Ever Christmas?"

"Too close to Forever Christmas, don't you think?"

True. "Evergreen Dreams?"

"I'll put that on the list for a possible yes."

Finally

Starr spoke the name into her cell phone, then tapped the device against her chin. "What was your mom's first name?"

"Everly. Why?"

"How about Everly's Evergreen Dreams?"

Waylon blinked, surprised by the surge of emotion that filled him. He blinked again, trying to keep the moisture at bay.

"Waylon?" Starr asked softly.

"I love it." He walked over and wrapped her in a hug. "It's perfect."

❄ seven ❄

This wasn't going to work.

Starr had known being a bridesmaid for her sister would be difficult, but she severely underestimated by how much. From the moment they had stepped into the bridal shop, Angel had ceased being the cheerful bride-to-be and turned into a stomping sea monster who spewed orders instead of nuclear radiation. Starr might've even seen puffs of smoke coming from Angel's nostrils as she declared the bridesmaids' dresses "totally unacceptable."

How on earth could anyone think the floor-length cranberry gowns with lace sleeves didn't fit a Christmas-themed wedding? Even Starr could begrudgingly admit all the bridesmaids made a stunning visual.

Too bad Angel wasn't satisfied.

Now the eight bridesmaids were being paraded in front of Angel wearing different gowns in order to soothe the savage beast that was the middle Lewis sibling.

"Doesn't she know the wedding is in two weeks?" Eve asked as she stood in a tea-length maroon chiffon dress.

Angel had nixed four of the new dress options with an emphatic no.

"I don't think she cares," Starr murmured back to Eve.

Woman after woman stood on the fashion podium, twirling before Angel and receiving a rejection. If Starr weren't directly involved, the ceaseless rotation of bridesmaids' gowns would be comical. Only this would be Starr's third time up on the podium. She was tired of switching dress after dress. The whole day annoyed every last nerve.

As the last bridesmaid flounced off the podium, Angel stalked over to the bridal consultant. "I need more dresses to choose from. None of these will work." She waved a hand in the direction of the dressing rooms, where the bridal party awaited their marching orders.

"All we have are the castoffs, Ms. Lewis. You have a lot of bridesmaids. The chances of having a matching design are slim. Are you sure the gowns you ordered won't work?"

Angel frowned, crossing her arms as she contemplated the consultant's words.

"I'll go talk to her," Eve muttered.

"Good luck." Starr watched as Eve neared Angel.

As the seconds ticked by in excruciating slowness, Angel grew more and more animated, flinging her arms in frustration. Eve leaned forward, continuing to speak quietly. Starr almost wished she'd speak up so the rest of them could hear. Finally, Angel grew still, then nodded her head. Eve motioned the store employee over, exchanging a few more words.

Starr watched as the consultant disappeared, and Angel sat back down on the couch. Eve walked back over to where Starr stood.

"What did you say?"

Eve folded her arms. "I told her to either go with the original order or let us all pick a dress the same shade. The store has quite a few castoffs in the particular red shade Angel wants."

"Good thinking. I hope that appeases her."

"Tell me about it," Eve groused. "I'll be glad when this is over."

"Me too. Nothing is like I hoped it would be." Standing in the dress had nearly reduced her to tears as Starr remembered the ease in which Ashton ditched her for Angel. Once again, Starr was found lacking.

Eve cocked her head to the side. "Did you think Angel would fall at your feet, begging for forgiveness and deeming you maid of honor?"

Starr snorted. "No, but I didn't think she'd turn into Bridezilla and torture us with fitting after fitting." Her feet were begging to come out of these heels.

"How do you feel about her and Ashton?" Eve studied Starr. "Did you ever tell her how you felt, or did you simply let it go?"

Starr had a bad habit of holding her hurts in and only sharing snippets of them. Did anyone truly understand her? She sighed as she thought of a way to respond to Eve.

"See, even now, you can't be honest about how you feel."

"I can." She straightened.

Eve's lips twisted into a smirk as if to say *Oh please*.

"I tell people how I feel."

"Okay. Let's see if we can prove it. I think you're a doormat."

Tears sprang to Starr's eyes, and she opened her mouth, then quickly shut it. She schooled her features, remembering they were in public. *No need to cause a scene.* She took a steadying breath. "I just want to keep the peace."

"Ugh." Eve shook her head in disappointment. "You can't even tell me I hurt your feelings."

"I, uh . . ."

"Starr!"

"What?" She held up her hands, even though she'd much rather shield her face and let a tear or two fall.

"This is exactly what I'm talking about. I purposely hurt you. Tell me how it feels. Don't bottle it up. It's not healthy."

She gaped at her oldest sister. "That was a test?"

"I said we were going to practice." Eve's hushed voice was harsh to Starr's ears.

"Maybe we can practice in private." She looked around at the other bridesmaids. Thankfully, they had all broken into groups and were having their own conversations.

The consultant returned and began handing out new dresses.

"We'll finish this later," Eve said sternly.

"Okay." Starr forced a smile onto her face and quickly ducked into her dressing room.

The consultant handed her a dress. A beautiful red gown with an empire waist, a V neck, and lace cap sleeves. Fortunately, Angel was having a church wedding and an indoor reception, so Starr wouldn't have to worry about freezing.

She slipped on the gown, then exited the fitting room. Eve came out of her room at the same time wearing the same style dress.

"I love this one. You?" Eve asked.

"Same. It's pretty and definitely a great shade of red."

One by one, the other bridesmaids came out wearing new gowns. Five of the dresses were floor-length and the same shade of red but with halter-top necklines. The last one had a tea-length strapless gown in the same shade.

"Come, ladies. Let's show the bride-to-be." The older consultant smiled, a matronly expression on her face as she waited for them.

Starr stood with Eve and twirled once more, rolling her eyes at Eve in conspiracy. Her older sister winked back as they faced Angel.

"Next." Angel swiped left with a motion of her hand.

They moved out of the way as the halter-top-wearing bridesmaids stepped forward.

"Last," Angel called.

Amber took her spot on the podium in front of Angel.

"Are there any more like this?" Angel waited expectantly.

"No, ma'am. This is the only one, but as you can see, it is the same shade as the others."

Angel pointed to the group of five. "What about that one? Any others?"

"No, ma'am."

Angel heaved a sigh. "What about that one?" She pointed toward Starr and Eve.

"No. Remember, these are all castoffs. We picked the ones that were the same color."

Angel drummed her fingers along the couch arm. "Fine. Amber, you're out."

Amber squeaked. "What?" She stepped off the podium, the tea-length gown flouncing with her movements. "What do you mean?"

"You don't match. You're the odd man out, so I have no choice but to remove you as one of my bridesmaids. Surely you understand?"

"But we've been friends since kindergarten." Her mouth dropped open.

Starr tensed, watching as the scene unfolded. Would Angel really kick her childhood BFF out of the wedding party?

"And we'll remain friends. I'll be in your wedding—"

"Oh no, you won't!" Amber scowled, then fled to her fitting room and slammed the door.

"Yikes," Starr muttered. She'd happily give up her spot as a bridesmaid if it meant she could avoid the rest of the drama.

Angel stood and walked over to Starr and Eve. "You two

will be my maids of honor. It'll be a great explanation for why you don't match the other girls."

"Angel!" Serenity placed a hand on her hip. "I'm supposed to be your maid of honor."

"But you don't match Starr or Eve."

"She can wear my gown," Starr quipped. "Or Amber can." Anything to get out of the wedding.

"Hmm." Angel tapped her chin. "That's actually a good idea."

"Now, Angel, you know Mom won't agree," Eve said.

Angel rolled her eyes. "It's my wedding."

"Exactly." Starr discreetly nudged Eve. "She's been best friends with Amber for as long as I can remember. Amber can have my spot."

"Does the gown even fit Amber?"

Starr kept her face from scrunching up. It had *better* fit.

Angel walked over to the dressing room, trying to coax a bitter Amber out from the other side of the door. Finally, she called Starr over and asked her to give the dress to Amber.

Starr put on her clothes and sighed in relief. In a few moments, the bridal nonsense would be all over. She could go back home and send out more résumés. Yesterday, she'd widened her search to the New England area. Still, not one response in her inbox. She was starting to become disheartened.

Lord, please help me. I can't live at home forever.

She peeked around the dressing room door, then grimaced. Amber's bosom was spilling out of the V neckline. If Angel didn't want gawking from the wedding guests, she'd need to find another gown for her best friend.

"What about her dress?" The consultant pointed to Serenity. "Can those two trade?"

"Let's try."

The girls came out with smiles on their faces. Relief filled

Starr. She didn't have to be in the wedding. She wanted to shout hallelujah and bow at Jesus's feet immediately.

She strolled over to Eve and gave her a side hug. "I'm so lucky."

Eve chuckled. "Until Mom finds out."

"Please, don't ruin this for me. I'm praying Mom will be okay with it."

"Not likely."

Starr sighed.

"Great." Angel clapped her hands together. "Everyone, these are the dresses." She met Starr's gaze. "Don't think the switch-eroo means you're out of helping me with the wedding favors."

Starr wanted to roll her eyes, but if she didn't have to be in the bridal party, she'd gladly make wedding favors.

"We have a lot of favors to assemble, and I need all hands on deck." Angel spoke to the room at large. "Don't forget, the wedding-favor social is tomorrow."

Starr made her way to the door, thankful the fitting was over, and glanced at her watch. Waylon should still be working. She could go over and see if the Christmas tree displays had increased foot traffic.

An hour later, she walked up to the shop and grinned. The trees looked wonderful from the outside. She made a note to order a sign with the new shop name. The bell above the door rang when Starr pushed it open. Last night, Waylon had purchased the new fixture along with the trees.

She paused in the doorway, taking in the scene before her. A few people milled about, while one woman talked to Waylon, holding an ornament in her hand. He met Starr's gaze with a smile and held up a finger, asking her to wait. She nodded, then moved about the store. The displays really changed the feel of the room, but they needed to do more. *What am I missing, Lord?*

Maybe the knickknacks would work better on separate shelves to hold them. Then they could decorate the shelves with lights and garland. She typed the note into her phone. Her eyes scoured the interior, looking for other changes they could make.

Perhaps a faux fireplace with stockings hanging?

Moments later, the store emptied, and Waylon walked over. "Hey, Starr. How was the fitting?"

"Great!" She gave an inward shake of the head. *A little less enthusiasm, girl.*

"Why's that?"

"I'm no longer a bridesmaid."

"Really?" His brows rose. "How did you manage that?"

Starr told him about the dress fiasco and how she volunteered to give up her gown.

"Very magnanimous of you. I'm sure you were heartbroken inside."

"You have no idea." She put a hand to her heart.

His lips twitched. "Does that mean no wedding-favor party or whatever Angel's calling it?"

"I wish." She pursed her lips. "Bridezilla said she needs all hands on deck, and I can't get out of that."

Waylon chuckled. "Then what time should I pick you up?" He took a step closer.

Her mouth dried at his nearness. "What about the store?"

"I'll close a little early."

Her pulse skittered as she took in a heady whiff of his cologne. Why did he smell so good? "Are you sure?" Her voice sounded muffled under the pounding in her ears.

"Very." He shifted closer and gently grasped her chin. "Starr?"

"Yes?" Her voice came out breathy as she instinctively rose up on her toes.

74

"I really want to kiss you." He dipped his head, his lips inches from hers.

"Oh good," she murmured, keeping her voice intentionally low. "It's not just my imagination."

"Not unless we're both dreaming."

"Pinch me after you kiss me."

Waylon closed the distance as his lips softly brushed hers. She sighed with pleasure. This was perfect. Not rushed. Not clumsy. *Nothing like Ashton's kisses.*

Starr pushed the thought aside, not wanting anything to distract her from the feel of Waylon's lips on hers. She clutched his arms, trying to hold herself up as her knees wobbled from the heady feeling rushing through her limbs.

Waylon brushed a kiss on her cheek and then moved back. "I've been wanting to do that since yesterday."

"Really?" She eyed him, stunned and a little dismayed she had nothing more coherent to offer.

"Really." He brushed her cheek with the back of his knuckles. "You're so beautiful, inside and out."

"Waylon . . ." Heat rushed to her cheeks. She didn't know if it was his touch or the kind words.

"It's true." He pulled back, his eyes dark with intensity. "Go out with me."

❄ *eight* ❄

Waylon's heart thudded as he waited for Starr's response. The way she'd kissed him back should've given him hope that a date would be accepted with enthusiasm. But the way her eyes widened made his heart clench. She was going to say no unless he could convince her otherwise.

"Nothing serious. I'm not asking for your hand in marriage." He winced. "Uh, not to say I wouldn't someday. I just mean it's a date. Only a date." He clamped his mouth shut, wishing he could take back all the words. All. Of. Them.

Why did she tie him in knots?

"Waylon, you know I'm only here for the holidays, right?" She bit her lip, her expression unreadable.

He'd seen that look before. Now if only he knew what it meant. "Yes, but nothing says you can't have fun on vacation. Pretty sure that's the point."

A wry grin tugged at her lips. "That's true."

"And I do think I'm pretty fun." *Please say yes.*

"You do, huh?"

He slid his fingers through hers. "Let me show you."

"Something tells me you're more trouble than fun."

"My fun only seems like trouble if you're scared." If she was, then maybe she really liked him. The kind of *really* that mattered in a relationship and led to a lasting commitment. The thought of long distance no longer scared him. Starr brightened his days, and if longevity was in their future, he'd welcome it. *Lord, please let it lead to forever.*

"Maybe I'm not scared but terrified," she whispered.

"Of what?" He carefully rested his forehead against hers after widening his stance. It was the only way to keep from getting a cramp in his neck due to their height difference.

"You."

Not what he expected. "I'm not scary. I can't even frighten anyone on Halloween."

She chuckled. "Be serious."

"All right then." He swallowed. "What about me scares you?"

"The way you make me feel."

His heart stuttered. Oh man, she had a way with words. "The way you make me feel makes me believe I can fly."

"Eventually that high will leave, and you'll go splat. Experience has taught me that."

Gruesome imagery. Another reason to give Ashton the cold shoulder. "Or you'll realize I'm the 'wind beneath your wings.'"

"Your one-liners are killer."

His lips twitched. "But I had you at hello, right?"

Starr shook with laughter.

"Told you I'm fun. Come on, take a chance. Go on a date with me. If you truly hate the experience, we won't do it again and will simply count ourselves friends."

"And if I like the date?"

"Then I'll keep asking you out until you decide I'm worth it."

"Worth what?"

"The risk." He kissed her on the lips and pulled away. "Because I already know you are."

She stared at him, a look of contemplation on her face. "Okay," she stated slowly. "I'll go out with you."

Yes! He bit the inside of his cheek to keep a full-fledged grin from breaking out. No need to make her run in the opposite direction. "How does Friday sound?"

"Good."

"Seven?" He stepped back and straightened, alleviating the ache in his back.

"I'll be ready."

He placed another kiss on her cheek, avoiding her lips on purpose. A few kisses and already he was intoxicated. "I can't wait," he murmured.

Her cheeks darkened, but she met his gaze. "Now let's talk business."

"If we must."

She shook her head in amusement. "I made some more notes."

"I'm sure you did. Let's go sit in the back. The new bell will let us know if anyone comes in."

"Okay."

Once they were settled in the office, Starr pulled out her cell. Her thumbs raced across her screen. Finding her information, she began to explain the changes she wanted to make to the shop.

Waylon watched her, mesmerized. When she was in business mode, self-assurance coated her every word as she gave directions and explained why she wanted to make a certain change. It was all he could do to focus on what she was saying and not get lost in studying her.

"Are you listening?"

He snapped to attention. "I am."

"What did I say then?" She folded her arms across her chest.

"That I need a new sign and logo and to put a wreath on the door."

"Lucky guess."

He chuckled. "I promise I'm listening."

"Well, you did look like you were concentrating, just not on what I was saying. More like studying?" She cocked her head to the side as if to do the same.

"I was focusing on not being distracted by your beauty."

Starr's lips quirked. "So cheesy."

"But you like it."

"Maybe."

He leaned forward and kissed her on the cheek. "I have a wreath I can go put on the door now. However, the logo and sign will take a bit."

She held up her laptop case. "I can do some mockups for you."

"You're a graphic designer now too?"

"Jack-of-all-trades, master of none."

He shook his head. "That, I doubt." He wrapped one of her curls around his finger. "Noel showed me one of your stories."

"What? Which one? When?" Her startled gaze flew to his.

The hairs on his arms raised. Obviously, this was an area he needed to be careful in. "It was in college. Or rather, we were in college, and your high school published the story."

"How embarrassing." She covered her face with her hands. "And why are you still holding my hair?"

"It's soft." The strands held a light citrus scent.

"Waylon?"

"Yes?"

"I need to be able to be your friend if our date doesn't work."

"It will."

She sighed, staring pointedly at the finger wrapped in her hair.

"Fine." He unraveled her hair, laying it across her shoulder. "I'll keep my distance, maintaining a mysterious aloofness that will have you wondering why we haven't committed to one another." He blinked. "I mean as boyfriend and girlfriend, not the covenant type of commitment." He stopped talking.

"I know what you meant." She studied him, uncertainty darkening her eyes. "You have to understand that once I get another job—"

Her eyes widened, and color leached from her face.

"What happened to your PR job?" he asked softly. He didn't want to spook her, because she obviously hadn't meant to let that slip.

Silence fell between them.

He maintained eye contact. *Lord, please help her to know I'm trustworthy. I won't judge her. I can listen.*

Finally, she said, "I was laid off." She shrugged. "Most expendable employee and all that."

"I'm sorry. Their loss."

"Pretty sure it's mine." Her eyes teared up. "Considering the severance package couldn't keep me in New York."

"Have you been searching for another job since Thanksgiving?" Why hadn't she told anyone? Surely her brothers would happily use their contacts to help her.

Then again, maybe that's exactly why she hadn't. Starr had always been fiercely independent . . . or at least the Starr from his childhood had been.

"I've applied to a ton of companies in the New England area. No such luck yet."

"What about DC?" His pulse pounded as he waited for her answer.

Would she consider moving here even though they hadn't

gone out on a date yet? Not that he would be the reason. Her entire family was down here.

"I assume I'll go back to New York." She looked down at her hands.

"What's in New York? Friends?"

"Well . . . I didn't have lots of friends. Just one or two co-workers I hung out with from time to time. Plus, I had to let my apartment go."

"But you always seemed to have so many friends growing up." What happened between the Starr from back then and the one he was getting to know now?

She shrugged. "New York is a little exhausting. No time for friends unless I wanted to forgo beauty sleep."

"So that's your secret."

She rolled her eyes, but her lips curved in a smile.

"Maybe DC could be a possibility then. Surely the pace here isn't as fast as New York."

She slowly nodded. "Maybe you're right."

Thank You, God.

"Enough about me." She waved a hand. "We need to finish getting the shop ready."

"All right." He stood.

"Waylon . . ."

"Yes?" He peered down into her eyes.

"Please don't tell anyone."

"I won't."

"Thank you." She smiled up at him with gratitude.

※ ※ ※ ※

"Listen up, everyone. The first party favor we're putting together is an ornament." Angel held up a sphere etched with *Ashton & Angel* and their wedding date. The round favor had been filled with something—Waylon couldn't quite make out what—and dangled from a red ribbon. "You'll fill each with one scoop of the red glitter and then one scoop of the silver glitter. Then add the top and attach a red ribbon to it."

Waylon stared at the materials laid out before him. When he'd offered to join Starr, he'd thought they'd be making one party favor for the large number of guests, then call it a day. The Lord knew making wedding favors for four hundred people was bad enough. Knowing there was more than one favor had him wishing for a dental appointment or any other torture preferably.

He glanced at Starr, sitting on his right. Her face was a perfect picture of calm and attentiveness. What he'd first thought was a practice in serenity he now suspected was an established façade. Did her family realize how awful this experience was for her?

Angel seemed to have no shame in stealing Starr's boyfriend—regardless of when and how he dumped her. And now to kick her out of the wedding party—no matter if Starr volunteered—and still expect her to help was beyond ridiculous.

"Once we've gotten all four hundred ornaments complete, we'll move on to the next favor." Angel continued.

One of the groomsmen groaned.

"Now, Carter, it won't be that bad. I fed you guys, after all."

"Yeah, tea sandwiches and fruit. Who can live on that?" Starr muttered.

Waylon smiled at her first show of irritation. "I don't know. Who?" he whispered, leaning toward her.

"Not me. If I'd known she'd be starving us and making us work so hard, I would've stopped for a burger."

"Only a burger?" He scooped glitter into his ornament.

"Add fries and a milkshake."

"What kind of milkshake?" His fingers kept bumping into each other as he attempted to tie a knot in the ribbon.

"Chocolate. Or peanut butter." She paused. "Do you need help?"

He groaned. "My fingers are too big to tie this in a knot."

She took the ornament from him and tied a bow in no time.

"How did you do that?" He gaped.

She shrugged. "Small hands?"

"How about this. I scoop and put the top on, and you tie the ribbons?"

"Deal."

"Thank goodness." He scooped the glitter into the next ornament. "For being so awesome, I'll buy you that victory meal. Maybe we'll hit up someplace like The Capital Burger?"

"Oh, yum! Their pickles are so good."

"Then it's a date." He paused. "Wait, no. We'll consider it a trial run since our date is Friday."

Starr chuckled. "We can go on more than one date, can't we?"

"Do you want to?" He lowered his voice to keep their conversation private. "I know you were hesitant to say yes in the first place."

"That's true. Maybe you're winning me over." She winked at him.

His heart thudded in his chest. A woman who could wink was dynamite. "Thank goodness. That means I can't go wrong on our Friday date."

"Oh, sure you can." Starr looked away as Eve asked her a question. Afterward, she turned back to Waylon, grabbing the made-up ornament.

"So, Ms. Lewis, will you be grading me?"

"All women do."

"Huh. Maybe that's why I've had so few dates."

Starr threw her head back and laughed. The sound reminded him of airy wind chimes. Chill bumps enveloped his arms despite his sweater, and his face flushed as a few members of the wedding party glanced their way.

Starr tied another ribbon. "Are you sure it wasn't the women that failed?"

"Men don't grade dates."

"Then how do you decide if you want to go out again?"

"Simple. If I still like her by the end of the night, I'll ask her on another date."

"Then you do grade dates."

"Uh-uh, I grade women." He winked. "But I'm smart. I do most of my recon before I even ask her out. If I ask, I'm about eighty-five percent sure it'll be a success."

"Then why so few dates?"

"Drat. You caught me."

She nudged him with her elbow. "Waylon, I'm just messing with you."

"I know." He threw another wink her direction and smiled as her cheeks bloomed with color—and not from her makeup.

Angel came to stand behind them. "Are you guys working together?"

Starr glanced over her shoulder. "He has two left thumbs."

"Men." Angel shook her head. "At least you've gotten quite a few done." She placed the ornaments into a bin, picking up the count from the ones already inside her container.

One hundred already? Maybe they really wouldn't be here all evening.

"Listen up, everyone. We're a quarter of the way through the ornament favors. Let's keep moving along."

Waylon winced at Angel's high-pitched voice. It zinged right through his frontal lobe. When she walked away, he leaned toward Starr. "Do you know how many different favors she plans on giving out?"

"Three."

He groaned.

"It could be worse."

"How?" He passed another ornament to Starr.

"She wanted the family to do everything. Her wedding planner suggested it would be a good way to save money since Dad put a cap on her expenses. He reminded her he has three daughters. I know she scoured the internet searching for deals on party favors and centerpieces."

"So we only have to do the favors?"

"*You* only have to. I'll be stuck for it all."

Judging from the expression on her face, Starr would be miserable every step of the way. Was it heartbreak or something else?

"Some return home, huh?" He softly nudged her arm with his.

"Amen," she murmured.

They continued their rhythm until Angel announced that all four hundred ornaments had been filled and tied.

Waylon sighed and stretched his arms out in front of him. "What else is Angel making you guys do?" He turned in his chair to face Starr. She really was beautiful.

Eve caught the movement, so he faced forward only to catch a smirk on Noel's face. Waylon remembered how the eldest sibling had asked him to be a friend. Would Noel be upset when he learned Waylon asked his baby sister out? Sitting at a table full of Lewis siblings was like being in a live exhibit.

Thankfully, her brothers and sisters seemed content to keep their mouths shut about all the attention Waylon paid Starr.

"All the bridesmaids—oh, wait, that's not me anymore." Starr's voice interrupted his musings. "Well, they, me, and my mom will be decorating the church and reception area. Angel has to put her degree to use."

"She does have a knack for decorating." At least the favors looked amazing. "Would I have seen something she's done? Not including this."

"Sure, if you follow designer magazines."

Which he didn't. "Not really my thing." He scrunched up his nose.

Starr chuckled.

"Is it weird, her marrying before Eve?" he asked quietly. Not the *real* question he wanted to ask, but it would do.

"No. She's always had a boyfriend. Frankly, I'm surprised it took her this long."

"She's what, twenty-nine?"

Starr nodded. "Just turned so last week."

"Are you two or three years younger?" He couldn't remember the age gap between all the siblings.

"Two."

"Then you're already twenty-seven?"

"Yep."

Then there was a six-year age gap between him and Starr. Not bad.

"You're the same age as Noel, right?"

"I am."

"Is that too big of a gap?" Starr studied him.

He smiled at her. "You know, I think it's just right."

"Okay," Gabe interjected, leaning across the table. "Enough with the googly eyes you two are making."

"Are you feeling left out?" Starr countered.

Waylon laughed, quickly covering it with a cough at Gabe's glower.

"I'm *fine*."

"Sounds like you're hangry," Starr surmised.

"You are too."

Waylon bit the inside of his cheek. Gabe sounded like a whiny kid who needed a nap.

"Complain to Angel," Starr shot back. "Maybe she'll take pity on you."

"Enough, children," Noel stated calmly. Noel met Waylon's gaze. "And maybe tone down the gag fest."

"I think they're sweet," Eve said.

Starr huffed. "You should all go back to your wedding favors and ignore us."

Waylon could hear the embarrassment in Starr's voice.

"Sorry." The Lewis siblings spoke in unison.

Waylon turned back to his station to focus. He'd have plenty of time to talk with Starr when her family wasn't around.

❄ *nine* ❄

Starr paused in front of the mirror that hung above the foyer table. She smoothed her backside, making sure her sweater-dress hem was at the appropriate thigh level. Her black tights would ensure she didn't have a Marilyn Monroe incident while on her date. Besides, it was way too cold to go barelegged. She moved her curls behind her shoulders, then leaned forward to check her makeup.

The doorbell pealed throughout the house.

Ready or not. She opened the front door and held back a dreamy sigh. "Hi."

Waylon grinned, adorable crinkles popping up at his eyes and gentle lines framing his mouth. His whole face transformed. Even though they'd kissed before she agreed to this date, she was very much trying to keep her heart from falling and her mind from committing.

So much of her life was up in the air, and Waylon . . . well, he was an unexpected detour from the frenzy but also deserved so much more than a person trying to leave town. Though she had been mulling over his suggestion of searching for jobs in DC, for some reason, staying in town had never been an option. While it would be nice to see her family more, would they really *see* her?

"You look fantastic," Waylon said.

"Thank you. I believe that was the look I was going for."

"Mission accomplished, though I doubt it took much effort."

"You are such a smooth talker." His flattery sent her heart fluttering every single time.

"You haven't seen anything yet." He twirled her around and brought her close in an embrace.

"You can dance?"

Waylon ran his knuckles down her cheek. "I was my sister's partner when she took ballroom dancing lessons for her wedding. She wanted to surprise her fiancé, who already knew how."

He stepped back and tucked their still-clasped hands into his coat pocket. "Let's rock."

"Where are we going?" Starr grabbed her purse with her free hand and followed Waylon outside to his car.

"Do you like surprises?"

"Good ones."

"Then you'll like this." He held the passenger door open for her.

Before long, they were on the Beltway headed toward Maryland. Their conversation flowed seamlessly as Waylon navigated toward their secret destination. Starr laughed as he told her about a woman who'd come into the store looking for candy canes that morning.

"She was adamant that I should be selling them since I'm a Christmas store."

"You don't have a single piece of candy or food there."

"Exactly! She told me the candy canes should be shelved with the ornaments."

"Why?" Starr shifted in her seat to view his profile better.

"She hangs them on trees."

"Oh. I've seen that in movies but didn't know people actually did that." Her mom would die of shock if any of her siblings dared hang anything other than sanctioned ornaments on her tree.

"Neither did I. She promptly scolded me, shaking her finger at me all the way to the door."

Starr chuckled some more. "You poor thing."

He turned, giving her a hangdog expression. "I'm traumatized. Don't I deserve some TLC?"

"You want a hug?"

"That's a start."

The smooth tenor of his voice and the hint of tease laced in the words sent a flush throughout her body. Would the effect he had on her be obvious if she took off her coat and rolled down the window?

"It's a good thing you're driving. You can't get us into trouble that way." She snuck a glance at him to gauge his reaction.

He stopped the car and pointed out the windshield. "There's always red lights."

This man!

He placed a kiss on her temple. "Totally worth the trouble."

A smile broke out unbidden and stayed on her face as they continued driving. Waylon kept the light conversation coming, punctuated with kisses when he had to stop at a red light. By the time he parked in the National Harbor parking garage, anticipation lit Starr's nerves.

"Are we here for dinner?" she asked as they walked along the sidewalk.

"After this first part."

"Which would be?"

Waylon held out his palm, and she slipped her gloved hand in his. "We're almost there. Be patient, beautiful."

"Okay." She sighed in contentment as they strolled the rest of the way.

Starr blinked in surprise as they entered the Gaylord National Resort. *What in the world?* There had to be some reason he was taking her to a hotel—other than the obvious, which made her feel guilty for even thinking it. Surely that wasn't why he'd brought her here.

She kept silent as he guided her past the check-in counters to a sign labeled *ICE!*

She gasped. "I completely forgot about this."

The hotel hosted an annual ice sculpture event. Each year, artists created different pieces of frozen art around a central theme. One year there had been sculptures of the Peanuts gang. Another year, Shrek had been the theme. Regardless, they always had two giant ice slides inside the exhibit.

"Have you been before?" Concern etched lines in his forehead.

"Never. You?"

"Nope." Happiness lit his warm brown eyes. "Something we can experience together."

"I heard it's freezing in there."

"Oh yeah, they maintain the temperature at a chilly nine degrees. Have to keep all the ice sculptures frozen."

Brr. Fortunately, she discovered that the entry fees gave them access to extra-thick jackets and beanies to prevent guests from feeling the freezing temperatures.

"Enjoy." The woman smiled as she motioned them forward.

Starr walked into the tunnel, then paused as Waylon ducked his tall frame to avoid hitting the ice ceiling. She laughed at the sight.

"Hey, not all of us are the perfect height to walk in here," he groused.

"Here you thought my five feet and one inch wasn't good for anything."

He stepped out of the tunnel, straightening as he rubbed the back of his neck. "I'd still rather be tall."

"At least I never hit my head on ceilings."

"If I knock myself out, just kiss me awake."

She nudged him and walked forward. "These are gorgeous."

Intricate sculptures decorated the sides of the room, leaving ample space to walk and stop to take pictures. There was even a sculpture in the shape of a photo frame.

"Excuse me, sir." Waylon flagged an onlooker. "Could you take our picture?"

"Sure." The man took the proffered cell.

Waylon came around the back of the photo frame and draped his arm around Starr's shoulders.

"Say cheese."

They repeated the phrase, and the man went on his way. Waylon showed her the picture. "Don't I look dashing with all this extra padding?"

Starr nodded. "It keeps you from turning into an icicle."

He snorted. "Can't have that. Are you going to go on the slide?" Waylon peered down at her.

"I think we should. You did promise me fun."

"That I did."

She climbed up the steps and waited for Waylon to sit directly behind her so they could slide down as one. *One . . .* Why did that make her think of marriage?

"Ready?" he asked.

Starr brushed her thoughts away. "Yes."

"Here we go."

Starr squealed as she slid down, a rush of cool air enveloping her. As she came to a stop, she realized she'd been giggling with delight.

"That was so awesome."

"Yeah, it was." Waylon got off the slide and offered her a hand.

She grasped it, letting him pull her up. Then Starr rose on her tiptoes and kissed his cheek. "Thank you so much."

"My pleasure." His eyes shone as though the words were true down to his core. "Come on. I hear there's a nativity scene in here."

"Yeah? This will be the most unique one I've ever seen then."

They oohed and aahed over other sculptures until they finally came to the nativity scene. "Oh wow," she whispered.

The elaborate detail in the sculptures was amazing. Were the artists believers? There seemed to be such care in their work. *Lord, thank You for the gift of Your Son.*

After a few more moments staring in silence, Starr turned to Waylon. "Thank you. This has been wonderful."

"I agree. Ready to go?"

Starr nodded. Waylon held her gloved hand as they made their way out of the *ICE!* venue and back toward the National Harbor.

"Want to go on the Ferris wheel?" She pointed to the Capital Wheel, lit up against the night sky.

Waylon glanced at his watch. "I made dinner reservations, and we'll be on time if we head there now."

"Got it."

He escorted her to one of the restaurants overlooking the Potomac River. Soon the hostess seated them in a booth showcasing a beautiful view of the harbor. A gigantic Christmas tree near the waterline shone with colored lights and ornaments for all to enjoy.

Starr glanced at Waylon. "Do you have any plans for Christmas?" She opened the menu and glanced at the offerings as she waited for Waylon to reply.

"Noel invited me over for dinner."

"Oh?" She peeked above the menu. "Hopefully Christmas dinner is better than Thanksgiving. After all, Angel will be on her honeymoon."

A shadow crossed his face. "Does that bother you?"

"No. It relieves me."

"Because you don't have to be around Ashton anymore?"

Her mouth gaped. "Is that what you think? That I want him back?"

"I don't know what to think." Waylon swallowed. "Do you?" he asked hesitantly.

"Not at all. He's not worth my time. I only pray he stays faithful to Angel."

"That's big of you."

She shook her head. "No. It's simply because she's my sister. I don't wish her ill. I'm not even mad about being dumped anymore. It's just . . . her lack of remorse is off-putting."

"Not the way she bosses everyone around?"

She laughed. "You really should have been there for the dress fitting. Talk about bossy."

Waylon laid his hand across the table, palm out. Starr placed her hand in his.

"I'm glad Ashton didn't break your heart. Plus, I'm relieved you don't want him anymore."

"How can I when my thoughts are on someone else?"

A slow smile covered his face, and Starr released a breath she hadn't realized she'd been holding. Waylon was kind, funny, and made her heart flutter with his lingering looks. Were they destined for a long-distance romance, or should she give moving to DC more consideration?

Lord, please show me what to do. I don't want to hurt Waylon, and I certainly don't want to jump all in to a relationship if I'm going to return to New York. Do You have any guidance? Any at all?

Starr bit her lip as the server showed up. They both placed their orders.

"So how would you grade this date so far?" Waylon asked.

"You get bonus points for originality. I can't believe you didn't buy movie tickets or something."

He shook his head. "You can't deliver cheesy lines in a movie theater. They frown upon talking."

"I may have heard that." She paused. "So far I'm thinking this is one of the best dates I've been on."

"What would make it better?"

"Hmm." She pretended to think. "Going on the Ferris wheel."

"What if I'm afraid of heights?"

"Are you?"

"No, but me and Ferris wheels don't get along."

Starr tried to hide the smile as she imagined what he could possibly have against the ride. "Is it going up that bothers you or going down?"

"More like having rickety cages rock as the spindle rotates. What if they drop? What if a strong gust of wind blows them sideways?"

She pointed out the window. "That's not a carnival ride. No way that's tossing anyone from side to side."

"So you're saying I should try it."

"I won't make you. But I hear you can take pictures there. Maybe that's our compromise."

Waylon sipped his water. "All right. I'll see how I feel. At the least, we'll get the picture."

The idea of having a professional picture of her and Waylon let the butterflies loose in her stomach.

"So besides helping me at the store and being Angel's wedding minion, what else are you doing?"

"I've hung out with a couple of friends from high school. Mostly, though, I've been looking for jobs and relaxing with other hobbies."

"Oh? What kind of hobbies?"

Her cheeks heated. "Writing stuff."

"You still write?" He arched an eyebrow.

"Yes, but just as a stress release." She didn't want him to know how much of her notebook she'd managed to fill. Waking up in the middle of the night the other day had worked in her favor. For some reason, words had been pouring out of her since she'd come back home.

"That's awesome. My hobbies are strictly on the TV."

"What do you and Noel do for fun?"

"Go to the sports bar, catch a game or two. But, you know, other than that, guys don't really hang out."

"Sure, sure."

They joked all the way through dinner and shared about themselves. Apparently, Waylon's brother-in-law was stationed overseas, so he didn't have any family around, which was why Noel had invited him over for Thanksgiving and Christmas.

"I bet you miss your mom."

He nodded. "So much. And at odd times. I got a little choked up when I saw her copy of *A Christmas Story* DVD in a random box at the shop. She loved that movie."

"Are you going to watch it this season?"

Waylon tilted his head, then shrugged. "I'm not so sure. I

can't decide if holding on to some of the traditions she had will make the grief worse or better."

She reached over and squeezed his hand. "Whatever you decide, I'll be there, if you'd like."

"I'd like that very much."

❄ *ten* ❄

Waylon flipped the sign from *Closed* to *Open*. He took a sip of his black coffee and sighed. Nothing like a cup to get him started and figuratively wipe the sleep from his eyes. He powered up his iPad to open the app to take payments from customers. Next, he clicked *play* on the Christmas playlist and smiled when music began pouring from the speakers.

Many customers asked him how he could listen to Christmas music 365 days a year. Truth was, he tuned the noise out most of the time. Christmas songs had become an everyday part of his life, and he no longer picked out individual artists. The musicians were all background noise to him.

The front door chimed. Waylon jerked as he saw who the first customer was. Ashton sauntered over to the checkout counter, removing his gloves at the same time.

Waylon took a long swig of his coffee before speaking. "Good morning." Whatever the reason for Ashton stopping by, Waylon would make sure he remained caffeinated and prayed up.

Lord, I don't know what's going on, but wisdom and Your guidance would be very much appreciated.

Angel's fiancé turned in a circle, examining the shop before stopping and facing Waylon. "Quaint."

Why didn't that sound like a compliment? "My mother certainly thought so." He stared pointedly at the man.

"I'm sure." Ashton flashed a smile that resembled ones used by politicians on Capitol Hill. "I thought I'd stop by and chat for a few." Ashton slapped his leather gloves against his palms.

Was that supposed to be intimidating? Because, as it was, Waylon fought the urge to grin at the buffoon before him. "You did, huh? Are you in need of some Christmas decorations?"

"Oh, please, no." His lip curled. "Angel already decorated my apartment. Fortunately, her décor is immaculate. I received many compliments from my colleagues."

Waylon nodded, not sure what to say to that. Besides, his mind was too busy scanning Ashton for a sneak attack. The man was up to something, that was certain.

"I actually came here to talk to you about Starr." Ashton leaned against the counter. "Angel told me about your date last night."

Waylon struggled to keep his face neutral. "How did Angel know?" He was pretty sure Starr wouldn't have talked to her sister about their outing. Their relationship seemed too strained for a gab fest over boys.

"Angel overheard Starr talking to Mrs. Lewis." Ashton shrugged.

"I see."

"I'm not certain you do, but you will." He flashed his teeth.

Waylon was very tempted to mar them.

"You see, Starr is a different kind of woman. I'm sure, in your dating experience, you've realized there are those you marry and others you . . ." Ashton's voice trailed off, innuendo in every aspect of his expression.

"Others you what?" Waylon enunciated each word, his

voice dangerously quiet. Hopefully Ashton heeded the warning in Waylon's body language, or he'd be grabbing Angel's fiancé by the collar.

"Well, you simply don't put a ring on their finger. Starr's that type. She's nice. Loyal, even. But she doesn't have what it takes if you have any kind of aspirations in life." Ashton took in the shop to his left, then his right before facing Waylon once more. "Then again, maybe this warning was for nothing."

First, the man insulted Starr, now his mother's shop? Waylon straightened to his full height. "Aren't you marrying Angel in a matter of days? Why do you care what Starr's up to?"

Ashton shrugged. "Listen, if you want to maintain a relationship with a woman who will only drag you down, by all means, it's your life. I just thought I'd give you a little friendly advice. That's all. No harm." Ashton held his hands up, offering a magnanimous grin.

"How big of you."

Angel's fiancé preened. "I do what I can."

Waylon was really beginning to hate this man's cavalier attitude. "Did you share your concerns with Angel?"

"No need to get her involved. I don't believe she'd understand about the women you marry and those you don't."

"Or could be she'd object to you talking about her sister in that way."

Ashton smirked. "Angel's very well trained. She knows better."

What's that supposed to mean? Waylon froze as his thoughts scrambled, trying to decipher the hidden meanings. Did Angel know how Ashton really was?

"Glad we had this chat," Ashton said, "but I need to get back to work."

Waylon nodded, keeping his mouth firmly shut. If God could somehow postpone the torture of running into Ashton again, all the better.

"Think about what I said—and if you're interested, I can introduce you to some quality ladies." With that, Ashton slipped his leather gloves on and walked out the front door.

A whoosh of air escaped Waylon as he let out the pent-up breath.

Lord, what in the world was that?

He knew better than to believe a single word out of Ashton's mouth. What he didn't understand was the intent behind it. Was Ashton simply trying to break him and Starr up? Or something else? Something much more concerning?

For once, Waylon wished he weren't tied down to the shop. He'd like nothing more than to go over to the Lewis home and talk to Starr. He grimaced. Could he even tell her what Ashton said?

Lord, I'm a little lost here. Help?

His cell rang, alerting him to a FaceTime request. "Joanna!" His chest filled with warmth as he stared at his sister's face.

"Hey, Waylon."

"How are you? The kids?" He sure missed his niece and nephew.

"We're all great. In fact, I wanted to tell you something." She grinned, and her light brown eyes twinkled with mischief.

He hunched over. "Are you moving back?"

Her mouth dropped open in surprise. "How did you guess?"

"Seriously, you really are?" At her nod, he whooped. "I was hoping you guys would return soon. Where will you be stationed specifically?"

"Andrews. We'll arrive in six months, so be ready for all the love from your niece and nephew."

"This is amazing news." He couldn't help but feel a little pang of regret as well. His mom wouldn't be around to see her daughter and grandkids return, and in such close proximity too. "I thought Nate would be stationed in Japan for at least another year."

"That was the plan, but he'll be replacing someone who had to retire unexpectedly. It's a blessing in disguise."

"Why is that?"

"Because I'm pregnant!"

His mouth dropped, closed, and dropped again. "Oh man, Jo. Congrats. Are the kids excited?"

"Carter is holding out judgment. He wants a little brother. Abby doesn't care."

"What about Nate?" His brother-in-law was pretty stoic, but he lit up around Waylon's sister.

"He's over the moon." A peaceful smile settled on her face.

"I'm so happy for you. You guys deserve so much good news." Maybe he was even a tad bit jealous. He wanted a family one day.

"I want you to be happy, too, baby brother. Are you?"

His lips quirked, thinking of Starr as she slid down the ice slide, laughing the whole way.

"Oh my goodness. What is up with that grin? Who is she, and when do I get to meet her?"

Waylon laughed. "Calm down. We've only been on one date."

"Her name?"

"Starr." He held his breath, waiting to see if Joanna remembered any of the Lewis siblings.

Her brow crinkled. "The Lewises' youngest girl?"

"Yes, but she's not a girl any longer."

"I guess not." Joanna shook her head. "She's in her twenties, right?"

"There's a six-year gap between us." Might as well just give his sister the answer she really wanted.

"That's not bad."

"I'm not worried."

Joanna laughed. "Then I won't. When do I get to see her again?"

"Good question. Right now, she's in between jobs, so there's no guarantee she'll be here in six months." That made him anxious, but he had to keep reminding himself that God would work it out.

"Oy. I'll be praying that changes."

"Thanks. I really appreciate it." He glanced at the door and then back to his phone. "Listen, could I get your opinion?"

"Sure."

Waylon hesitated. What if he told Joanna what Ashton said and his insinuations made her think negatively about Starr? That's the last thing he wanted.

"Never mind."

"Are you sure? Sounds like you have something weighing on you."

"I do. Could you just pray for wisdom for me?"

"Of course."

"Thanks, Jo."

"Anytime."

Movement out of the corner of his eye brought his head up. "Hey, I think I'm about to have a customer."

The door chimed.

"Okay, I'll talk to you later."

He ended the call. "Welcome to Everly's Evergreen Dreams. If you need help in finding anything, please let me know."

The older woman walked right up to Waylon. "Thank you so much. I've passed this shop so many times, and now just seemed like the perfect time to come in."

"I'm glad you stopped by."

She rummaged through her purse and pulled out an old ornament shaped like a stocking. "By any chance, would you have something similar and customizable?"

"Actually . . ." He smiled and gestured for her to follow.

Around the checkout counter, along the wall, were miniature stockings, which could be stitched with a personalization. He could add a string to turn it into an ornament.

Waylon explained his idea to the woman. "What do you think?"

"It's perfect." She clapped her hands together, eyes brimming with joy. "How long have you been here?"

"Well, I took over this year." He paused, a pang in his heart. "But my mom ran the store for about twenty years I'd say. She passed away recently and left the store to me." He slid his hands into his pockets. "Now I'm hoping to do the same to any future children I may have."

"What a legacy. Thank you for sharing that with me."

He nodded. "Thank you for listening." He pointed at the stocking. "What should I stitch on here?"

"Blackwell. It's my last name. My husband will just adore this."

"Give me a moment, and I'll be right back out." By the time he embroidered the stocking, added a red string, and handed it over, Waylon felt a lightness in his chest he hadn't felt before.

At first, working in the store was bittersweet, then bitter, and finally, determination had set in. Making sure his mom's store survived her death became Waylon's mission. Today was the first time feelings of true ownership had filled him. Turning the miniature stocking into an ornament for the customer gave him a sense of pride he hadn't felt the past six months. Maybe, just maybe, he could run the store without wishing for his past.

* * * *

Waylon tapped his fingers against the tabletop. Noel was ten minutes late to the restaurant. Maybe he should text him and cancel their meet up. It would be weird telling Starr's brother about her ex anyway. He groaned.

Lord, I don't know what to do with this information. Should I just let it go? Talk to Starr about it? Share it with Noel? He grimaced. If someone shared something similar with him about his sister, he'd be liable to hunt the guy down. Which wouldn't solve any problems.

So, yeah, maybe he'd made a mistake in contacting Noel.

"Hey, man. Traffic caught me."

Waylon looked up as Noel took a seat across from him. "No worries. I figured something came up."

Noel shrugged out of his suit jacket and draped it on the back of his chair. He faced Waylon. "I'm surprised you're not out with Starr."

"We're getting together Monday night." Because seeing her twice in a row seemed a little pathetic . . . but, honestly, was what he wanted.

"I'm glad."

"Are you? I know you wanted me to be a friend but not sure romance was what you had in mind."

Noel studied Waylon for a moment. "You're my friend. I trust you and know you wouldn't do anything to give me a reason to call the cops. You two are my favorite people, so, yes, you have my blessing."

Why did his skin feel tight? "Have to admit, I wish you'd threaten me or something."

Noel grinned. "I can certainly do that, but I really think you two are a good fit."

"What do you think of Ashton and Angel?" He held back a grin at his friend's scowl.

"I honestly don't know how the dude managed to date two of my sisters. I thought they were smarter than that."

"Then you don't like him?"

"Not at all. He's pretentious, arrogant, and—" Noel stopped himself. "I just pray he's good to Angel."

Waylon tapped the table and took a sip of his Coke.

"What? You have that look."

"What look?" Waylon had a pretty good poker face. But right now, stress clung to him, making it more likely for him to show his emotions.

"That look that says something's bothering you."

"Possibly."

"Is it the shop?"

"No."

"Sister's okay?"

"Yeah. She's actually moving back next year." He'd be able to be around family once again. *Thank You, Lord.*

"Good."

Waylon either needed to spill his guts or change the subject so Noel would stop chasing the white rabbit.

"Spit it out, Emmerson."

"Ashton came by to see me."

"Why?" Noel arched an eyebrow.

"Warn me against Starr."

"Are you serious?"

Waylon nodded. "Said I should look for someone else."

"Unbelievable." Noel shook his head, a look of disgust on his face. "He didn't want her, but heaven forbid if someone else does."

"You think that's all it was?"

"Without a doubt. I know guys like him. They can't stand to see someone else happy. Especially if they had a hand in them being miserable. Probably wanted to gloat over her sad single status at the wedding."

Waylon sat back, his shoulders sagging. "That makes sense." Even explained the lies Ashton had made up.

"Did he say anything else?"

"Nothing important."

Noel eyed him warily. "I'll take that to mean I don't want to know."

An uneasy chuckle fell from Waylon's lips. "Pretty much."

"Don't let him get to you. Continue treating my sister right, and all will go well for you."

"Ah, there's the threat."

Noel smirked. "Feel better?"

"Actually, I do."

His friend laughed.

They caught up on each other's business as they ate. Eventually they parted ways, and Waylon walked to where he'd parked his car. Noel had put him at ease, but Waylon still wondered what Ashton was up to. Hopefully he wouldn't spread his poison to Starr.

Waylon got into his car and pulled out his cell phone.

> **Waylon**
> Had dinner with your brother. Wish it had been your pretty face across from me.

He blinked in surprise as it chimed immediately.

> **Starr**
> His face is pretty enough.

He laughed.

Waylon
Nah. Not my type. 😉

Starr
I don't blame you. He snorts when he laughs really hard and always takes the last piece of food.

Waylon shook his head.

Waylon
So what are your faults?

Starr
I have none. Didn't you see the halo above my head?

Waylon
Is that what that was? I thought it was the glow from your beauty.

Starr
Smooth, Waylon, real smooth.

Waylon
It comes naturally.

Starr
Somehow, I doubt that. Tell the truth. You look these lines up online.

Waylon
I will never divulge my secrets.

❄ *eleven* ❄

Mmm. Starr took another bite of her mother's pumpkin bread. The added nuts and pumpkin seeds made her want to wiggle with happiness.

"I take it New York doesn't have pumpkin bread." Amusement laced Mom's words.

"Sure they do. Just not as good as yours."

Mom beamed. "I've missed you."

"I missed you too, Mom." Over two weeks of being home had changed Starr's original attitude about coming to DC. No, she hadn't found another job yet, and she hadn't submitted any of her applications she'd begun to fill out for jobs in DC, but she also didn't feel so blue about being jobless. Being at home and surrounded with family—maybe minus Angel—had relaxed Starr. Waylon also had done a lot to bring a smile to her face.

Why hadn't she done a better job at keeping in touch with her mom? Her brothers and sisters? In the beginning, Starr had assured herself they wouldn't miss her. They all had careers of their own, and the lack of calls and texts seemed to affirm that belief. Now Starr could admit that keeping in touch went both ways. *I'll do better from now on.*

"Are you going out with Waylon again?" her mom asked slyly.

"I am." The thought of him had her lips itching to curve in a smile, but the way her mom watched like a hawk had Starr biting another piece of bread instead.

"He's a good boy."

"Pretty sure he's too old to be called a boy."

Mom placed a hand on her hip. "Considering I remember him as a boy, that's what he'll always be to me."

Starr shook her head. Her mom liked to remind all of her siblings that no matter how old they were, they would always be her babies. Guess that applied to Waylon too. Starr finished off her pumpkin loaf and reached for her coffee.

The sound of footsteps caught Starr's attention, and Angel's frame appeared in the kitchen doorway. "Morning, everyone."

"Morning," Starr and her mom replied in unison.

Lord God, please take these hostile feelings away. Help me forgive her.

"Oh, you made your pumpkin loaf, Mom?"

"I sure did."

"Don't you know I can't eat fattening stuff right now?" Angel's nose scrunched up. "Surely you have some fruit or something healthy?"

Starr rolled her eyes and sipped her coffee. If Angel was going to bring her drama with her, Starr would need all the caffeine in the house to keep her mouth shut.

"How about an egg-white omelet, sweetie?"

"Perfect." The look on Angel's face made Starr think of a peacock spreading its feathers. Her sister took the barstool next to her at the kitchen island. "So, Starr."

"Yes?" Was it the coffee or Holy Spirit's help keeping annoyance from covering her words?

"About the whole bridesmaid incident."

Out of the corner of her eye, Starr saw her mom perk up. Dread pooled in her stomach.

"They found another gown like the one you tried on."

"Oh yeah?" *Lord, help.* Her breathing grew shallow as the implication sank in.

"Which means you can be my maid of honor again. Now I'll have three." Angel clapped her hands, as though life was suddenly perfect. "Plus, Ashton will be happy. He didn't want to get rid of one of his groomsmen."

"Oh." What else could Starr say?

"Here's what I need you to do. Go to the shop and make sure the gown fits perfectly. Then go to the shoe store. They have a few pairs of the bridesmaids' shoes in different sizes. I couldn't remember what size you wore, so they're holding a few choices for you."

So that was it? Starr was a bridesmaid—no, maid of honor—again? "Oh."

Angel checked items off in her cell phone's to-do list. "Last thing, I want you to make a toast at the rehearsal dinner."

She blinked. "Excuse me?"

"All the maids of honor are doing one."

Just great. How am I supposed to say something nice?
Because she's your sister.

Starr's shoulders dropped. "Fine."

"Perfect. I think that's all." Angel turned to leave.

Starr grabbed Angel's wrist, then stared down at her hand, stunned by her own movement.

Angel arched an eyebrow. "Do you need something?"

Starr took a deep breath. "Do you really think I'm the best person to say a toast?" She lifted her gaze, meeting Angel's startled eyes.

"You're my sister." Angel genuinely sounded surprised.

Though why shouldn't she? They *were* sisters, but so much

111

had passed between them, both said and unsaid. "I'm also the sister who dated your fiancé for six months."

"That's ancient history."

"Why? Because you said so?" Starr's jaw tightened.

"Now, girls."

Her mom's lips were pursed, arms folded. Of all the times to step in, she chose now?

"Mother, could you please excuse us?" Angel grabbed Starr's hand and pulled her out of the kitchen, across the hall, and into the living room.

She let go of Starr's arm and folded her own across her chest. "Are you *seriously* still upset?"

Starr gaped.

"I thought you were dating Waylon. I figured you were finally moving on and over your pining for Ashton."

Starr sputtered while Angel continued talking, a look of pity on her face. "He's my soul mate. You two weren't right for each other."

"On that I can agree with you one hundred percent." Starr's heartbeat raced as her skin heated from head to toe. Words she'd repressed for far too long spewed from her mouth. "Any man who would dump one sister for another is not one I want in my life. I've never *pined* for Ashton. What upsets me"—she took a step forward, pointing a finger at Angel—"is that you, *my own sister*, showed *no* remorse. None!"

"Ashton and I had a connection, Starr. What was I supposed to do?"

"Talk to me! Ask me if I'd be okay with it. Or at least have the decency to wait more than a couple of hours before going out and skipping off into the sunset holding hands as if you didn't just stick a knife through me."

"I was upset for you. Look how long it took you to date again."

Starr huffed. "Really, Angel? Are you that dense?"

"What are you talking about?"

"Waylon isn't the first guy I've dated since Ashton. He just happens to be the first one I think could lead to more."

"Then what is your deal?"

"You! You're my problem. You never said sorry. You never came and talked to me or explained how you could do something like that. Now you expect me to celebrate your nuptials to that slime? It's completely preposterous."

"If that's how you feel, then maybe you shouldn't be my maid of honor." Angel sniffed, tilting her nose in the air.

"Thank goodness. That sounds like the best suggestion yet."

Angel's eyes widened. "Fine," she snapped. "I didn't want you in it anyway. Mom made me."

"Real adult of you."

Angel's lips bunched as if she wanted to say something but somehow restrained herself. Which kind of surprised Starr. Since when did Angel have any kind of filter?

Starr turned to leave, but Angel's voice stopped her.

"If you aren't in the wedding, don't bother showing up."

She whirled around. "You're banning me from your wedding?" Did her heart just stop, then start up again?

"What do you care, considering how you feel about Ashton?"

"You're still my sister." That's what she'd been trying to get Angel to see. Sisters didn't do that to one another.

"If our familial connection meant so much to you, then you wouldn't have a problem being my maid of honor or making a simple toast."

Argh! Starr's breathing came in spurts. She was so tired of Angel's emotional blackmail. She would not kowtow to it again. Never again.

"As you wish." Starr stalked out of the living room, grabbed her purse from the foyer, and marched out of the house.

* * * *

Starr walked down the hallway leading to Waylon's apartment. He'd kindly texted her his address after she nixed his offer to pick her up. She'd spent the past few hours walking around DC, then headed to the mall before calling an Uber to take her to Waylon's place.

Before she could knock, her cell rang in her purse. She frowned at the unknown number flashing on the screen.

"Hello?"

"Yes, this is Dana Barry calling for Starr Lewis."

"Speaking."

"Ms. Lewis, I'm the executive assistant for David and David. We received your application and would like to schedule you for a phone interview."

She drew in a sharp inhale. "That would be wonderful." She winced. *Too eager?*

"Fantastic. Is Wednesday at nine a.m. too soon?"

"No, that's just fine." She wanted to jump up and down but settled for shimmying instead.

"Is this the best number to reach you?"

"It is."

"Then Mr. David Jr. will contact you at the scheduled time. If you pass the interview, I will schedule an in-person interview for you in front of the board."

Oh wow. Their process sounded expedient. But that was to be expected from an NYC company. "Thank you."

"You're very welcome. Have a good evening."

Starr was still staring at her cell when the door to Waylon's apartment opened.

114

Waylon's smooth voice broke her reverie. "Are you okay, Starr?"

Her mind tried to switch mental compartments, but all she could think of was what if David & David offered her a job? How could she leave Waylon behind for a job?

"Starr?"

"Sorry." She smiled, putting her cell back into her purse. "Phone call threw me, and my brain is trying to catch up." She walked into his apartment, discreetly checking out the interior. Well, not too discreetly, considering she did a three-sixty to take in the décor and furnishings. "Nice place."

The dark gray sofa had been outfitted with black throw pillows and faced a TV. She pointed to the flat screen. "Think that's big enough?" Had to be at least sixty inches.

"'Course not, but don't change the subject. Why are you upset?"

She frowned. "I had a not-so-nice conversation with Angel."

"I see." Waylon's steady gaze studied her as if trying to read her thoughts. "Do you wanna sit?"

She nodded.

"Can I get you something to drink?"

"No, thanks." Should she tell him about the job interview? *No need.* If she didn't get it, then telling him now would only worry him unnecessarily.

"Do you want to share what was said or talk about something else?"

"I really don't know." She tugged on the end of her hair. "I've never really talked that way before, and part of me thinks I should apologize. She told me not to come to her wedding."

"Whoa. Are you serious?"

"Yes," she whispered as her eyes filled with tears, her vision clouding. "That's not what I wanted. I just wanted an apology."

"That's understandable." Waylon shifted, threading his fingers through hers. "Did she apologize?"

"No. Told me I should stop pining for Ashton." She gave a snort of disgust. As if she pined over that two-bit cheater.

"Wow." Waylon squeezed her hand. "I guess she thought I was chopped liver, huh?"

Starr chuckled. "No, she thought you were the reason I stopped pining."

"Am I?" he whispered, his gaze darting to her lips and back to her eyes.

"I stopped long ago. But you're the reason this season actually feels like Christmas. The wonder of it all. The beauty in every moment." Her cheeks heated. That was way too much.

Waylon's finger drew a line down the side of her cheek, eliciting shivers in its wake. He leaned forward and pressed his lips to hers in a movement born of greeting, comfort, and passion. Starr met each kiss with enthusiasm until the temperature around her reached epic proportions. She broke off the kiss and scooted backward, widening the space between them.

"Sorry," he murmured.

"Me too," she mumbled past the fingers pressed to her lips. She dropped her hand. "Maybe we should leave your place and go somewhere else?"

Waylon nodded. "Good idea." He strode to the closet near the door and grabbed a jacket, shrugging the material over his shoulders. "Have you done all your Christmas shopping?"

"No. I have to watch my pennies, so I'm still trying to figure out what to get everyone." And wondering if she should come clean before they questioned why their gifts were obviously cheap.

"How about we finish that list of yours?"

"All right." She followed him out the door, standing by as he turned the lock.

He held out his hand, and they strolled down the hall. He pressed the down button on the elevator. "Maybe you should get Noel a tie. You can never have too many in the bank world."

She scrunched up her nose. "I usually get my dad a tie."

"Hmm. Maybe switch it up. Would your dad like the surprise?"

Starr thought about it. He never seemed too enthused about ties, so maybe buying something more thoughtful would work. "I think he might."

Waylon nodded. "I know the perfect store. We could probably get something for everyone."

"Where is this mysterious place?"

"A couple of blocks away if you don't mind the walk."

"I don't."

They strolled hand in hand down the sidewalk, passing other people out shopping. "Did you finish all of your shopping already?"

"Mm-hmm." He peered down at her. "Had to shop early so Joanna and the kids would get their gifts on time in Japan."

"Oh wow. Was that expensive to ship?"

"Not really. They have a military address, so it's like shipping to somewhere in the States." He pointed to a store. "That's where we're going."

He held the door open for her. She crossed the threshold, inhaling the scent of cinnamon. "Oh, Waylon. We need to get a Christmas tree scent for your shop."

"Actually, my mom had one of those warmers. The bulb was out, but I replaced it just this morning. Come by and all your nostalgia senses will be tingling."

She laughed. "Sounds perfect."

"Look at this." Waylon held up a tumbler. "Maybe for Gabe."

"That joke is perfect." She'd had to tilt her head to read it, but it definitely fit Gabe's humor.

"One down, many more to go." Waylon quipped.

"Oh, I see something for Eve." She rushed forward and picked up the red beaded earrings. "She'd look beautiful in these."

Waylon reached over her shoulder and picked up a bracelet. "Maybe this for Angel?"

Her bottom lip trembled, but she nodded, adding it to the collection in her arms.

"I can carry some of those for you."

"You don't mind?"

He shook his head. "That way I can still hold your hand."

Starr's heart dipped. How could she go back to the city as if she hadn't met the most perfect man for her?

❄ *twelve* ❄

Everly's Evergreen Dreams, this is Waylon speaking."

"Waylon Emmerson?"

Waylon quirked an eyebrow, glancing at the caller ID. *Hmm.* An unknown number. "Yes, sir."

"I'm Trent Blackwell. My wife was recently in your shop and told me how quaint and adorable it was. Her words, not mine."

Blackwell. Stocking ornament. "I remember her." He chuckled. "Glad she enjoyed her visit. I always aim to please."

"I hope you mean that. It would make her day if I purchased the shop."

"Excuse me?" Waylon flopped onto his office chair and ran a hand over his face.

"I'm sorry. There's probably a better way to do this." Mr. Blackwell cleared his throat. "I should've come by with my card all proper-like. Excuse my impropriety. My wife is currently out of the house, and I thought I could conduct some business before she returns."

Waylon shook his head, trying to follow the conversation. "Mr. Blackwell, my business isn't for sale." Not to mention, how did one go from buying an ornament to wanting the whole store?

"Come now. Surely there's a price that would make you happy. I looked up retail space in the area, and I think an offer of 1.5 million would be just."

"Mr. Blackwell . . . did you say 1.5 million *dollars*?" His mouth dried, and sweat beaded above his upper lip.

"Yes, Mr. Emmerson. My wife really wants to own your store."

Waylon slid a palm down his pant leg. "I'm not quite sure what to say."

"Will you think about it? If you give me your email, I can have my lawyer send all the pertinent paperwork."

"Uh . . ." *Think, man.*

"Your email, Mr. Emmerson?"

"Right." Waylon spelled out the address, his mind still trying to keep up with the conversation.

"Great. I'll have him send the information over to you this afternoon. My lawyer's name is Simon Prichard. And please, Mr. Emmerson, please think about this. If you're willing, I'd like the contract to be underway before Christmas. It would make a wonderful gift."

"Understood." That's about the only thing his mind was willing to comprehend.

"Good day."

Waylon stared at the office phone for what felt like hours but was probably only mere minutes. *Okay, seconds.* He rubbed his chin. What was he supposed to do? Never in a hundred years had selling his mother's place entered the realm of possibilities. Yet the thought of having a million in his pocket appealed. He could easily fund a nonprofit and work with youth like he had dreamed about.

Lord God, I'm absolutely stunned. I have no idea what to think or what to do.

He inhaled and exhaled slowly as he worked to calm his

mind and to focus. *This has such huge ramifications, Lord. I don't want to choose a path that would lead me outside Your will. Please give me direction and a clear choice that brings such a peace I know it can only be You leading me. In Jesus's name, Amen.*

Joanna. He needed to talk to his sister. If Waylon sold the store, splitting the money in half with his sister would be the right course of action. Granted, the store was in his name only, but Joanna had an investment in the place, as she sold her handmade ornaments. Plus, he was sure Mom would want it that way. If he sold the shop, how would his other wholesalers make up those sales? They wouldn't have half a million dollars to cushion their account like Joanna.

A glance at the clock and some mental time zone conversion told him his sister was most likely reading for bed. Maybe she could spare a moment to talk to him.

"Hey, baby brother. What a timely phone call. I just ended a chapter."

"God knew I needed your undivided attention."

"Give me a second."

He heard muffled talking. Presumably Jo talking to her husband.

"Okay, I'm back. What's so pressing?"

Waylon told Joanna about the offer.

"Are you serious?"

"Unless he's pranking me, deadly."

"Oh wow, Waylon. What are you going to do?"

"What are *we* going to do?"

"Sweetie, I love that you'd include me, but the store is all yours. You have my blessing to do what you think best."

"Really? You don't have any strong feelings one way or the other?" He was kind of banking on her input.

"Waylon, this was *Mom's* store."

"Exactly."

"No. I mean it was *hers*. Not yours, not mine. You didn't grow up dreaming of owning a Christmas store that catered to clients 365 days a year and neither did I."

"Obviously, but don't I owe it to her memory to keep it?"

"Waylon, there are other ways to remember her."

"Right." But imagining her in the store, remembering times they'd laughed, made her life seem more permanent than the fleetingness of death. He pinched the bridge of his nose.

"Are you sure you know that?"

He sighed, and Joanna chuckled.

"I'll take that as a no."

"I don't just want to remember her, Jo. I want to honor her."

"Bro, you've always done that. I'm sure every single day you wake up and use those wonderful manners she taught us. Although, I'm also sure you use them to charm the ladies—or rather, *Starr*."

His mouth quirked. "She may have called me charming once or twice."

"See? The lessons Mom instilled in you, in me, they live on."

He. Would. Not. Cry. "You really don't care what I do?"

"No, but thanks for thinking of me."

He opened his mouth to tell her he'd split the money but stopped himself. If he did sell the store, he'd surprise her with her half for Christmas. "Could you pray I make the right choice then?"

"Done."

"Thanks, sis."

"You're welcome. Now I gotta go. The heroine screamed

bloody murder before the chapter ended, and I need to know why."

He laughed. "Enjoy. Please tell everyone I said hi and I love them."

"Love you too."

He heaved a sigh. Waylon had hoped a conversation with his sister would ease the burden, only the weight of the decision weighed heavier. He stood, stretching the cramps out of his back and neck. As much as he wanted an answer right now, readying the store for the day took precedence. This dilemma would have to wait until after work. Maybe Noel could recommend a good lawyer to look over the paperwork to ensure the contract was a sound business deal.

Yeah, I'll ask Noel.

* * * *

Waylon strolled through Cornwall & Lewis toward Noel's office. Noel had told him to stop by before Waylon headed home for the day. Fortunately, the bank had its own parking lot, which allowed Waylon to avoid the terror of finding parking in DC.

A quick look around let him know Noel's assistant had already left. He rapped on the door and waited.

"Come in."

Waylon smiled at his friend. "Thanks for letting me stop by."

"No problem." Noel stood and walked around his desk, slapping Waylon on the back. "I took a look at the email and attachment."

"Oh, I figured you'd have a lawyer look at the contract."

"I did. Our in-house guy did it as a favor. Of course, I was curious about the financial portion."

123

Waylon sat down in the chair across from Noel. "What do you think?"

"I think it's a solid offer." Noel sank back into his chair. "You going to accept?"

"I don't know."

"Well, it's a good deal, and our lawyer says he couldn't see any issues, unless you want to negotiate or add your own terms."

"Appreciate your help with this." Waylon rubbed his chin, his thoughts going a mile a minute.

"I gotta ask. Does Starr factor into your decision?"

"Not really." He winced. "I mean, I don't see how this could make a difference to her one way or the other."

"You never know unless you talk to her about it."

Waylon sighed. "I've told you and Joanna. I think I'll limit who knows to you two for now."

Noel arched an eyebrow, twirling his pen between his fingers. "I'm surprised you haven't prayed about it."

"I have." Waylon met his friend's gaze. Just because he'd prayed didn't mean an answer had come right away.

"Did you hear from Him?"

"Not yet. I don't have a clear yes or no, but I know He'll prepare me for whatever the answer will be." Waylon sighed, leaning back in the chair. "Part of me hoped you'd say the deal was bad so I could hard pass. Now . . ." He shrugged.

"Now?" Noel eyed him.

"Now I need to keep praying. Ask God for clarity and peace, then trust He'll provide those."

Noel nodded slowly. "Praying is easy, but I've always found listening to be the hard part."

Wasn't that the truth. How many times had Waylon prayed in the past, then doubted the answer because it didn't come in some loud booming voice or obvious sign? "Any tips for that?"

"Line up what you know about God with what the Bible says. Outside of that, I don't think individual decisions are always a specific yes or no from God."

Waylon threw his friend a skeptical look.

Noel chuckled. "What I mean is I don't believe the decision will bring us outside the will of God. What might is if we don't do the steps of coming to Him first, laying out our desires, and accepting His will as supreme. That's the real issue. If He has a specific direction for us, I believe we'll know. Like that peace you spoke of. Sometimes answers come from His still, small voice, dreams, or your wiser friends." Noel smirked.

Waylon laughed. "Yeah, that same friend told me to pray."

"Well, there you go. God is obviously the answer."

Waylon shook his head.

"I know you want to keep this on the hush, but maybe consider bringing Starr in." Noel's brow furrowed. "I'm sure you'd want input on if she ever decided to move back to DC. If you two get serious, you'll need to start working as a unit instead of keeping your lives separate."

Wow. Hadn't Waylon asked Starr to think about coming back to DC? "You're right. I would want to be included in that decision."

"Good. I'd like to think this relationship between you has potential and you aren't doing a cliché holiday romance."

"I'm not cheesy like that."

Noel rolled his eyes. "I heard enough listening to you two at Angel's wedding-favor social. You're lovestruck."

Waylon wanted to laugh, but considering how happy he was whenever Starr was around, Noel probably wasn't that far off. He stood. "I'm going to go before you can lecture me more on your sister."

"Coward."

A bark of laughter flew from his lips. "Call me what you want. But keep in mind, I'm not answering to that."

"Yeah, we'll see if that's the case if my dad decides to get involved in the conversation."

A shudder ran through Waylon, and Noel doubled over laughing.

❄ *thirteen* ❄

The phone rang, showing a New York number on the caller ID. Starr blew out a nervous breath and answered with a cool and composed greeting. She'd prepped all yesterday, taking her Tuesday to make sure she could come up with rehearsed answers for interview questions while still sounding authentic.

As the interviewer asked her question after question, Starr's nervousness slowly abated. She had this. She knew what she brought to a team and why David & David should employ her.

"If we were to hire you, would you be able to start the day after New Year's?"

"Yes, that's perfect." Then she could return to New York, and no one in her family would ever know she'd been laid off.

"Fantastic. We still have some other applicants to question over the next two days. You'll hear from us by December twentieth if an in-person interview needs to be set up."

She bit her lip. "I'm in DC for the holidays, and my sister's getting married Christmas Eve." Not that she was invited any longer. "Would it be possible to do a video interview?"

"I'll make a note, but the hiring official will make that

determination. Please be aware, you may still have to come up here in order to be considered."

"Yes, sir. I understand."

"Have a good day, Ms. Lewis."

"You as well."

She hung up the phone and stared.

"You're looking for a new job?"

Starr squealed and jumped up. She whirled around, hand on her chest as she gaped at her brother. "What are you doing here? Aren't you supposed to be working?"

"Really?" Gabe folded his arms across his chest. "You can't deflect." He jerked his chin in her direction. "What's going on with your job?"

"Nothing. I'm just looking for a new one." She stared at the spot above his head.

"Why?" He drew out the word as if to suggest she was doing something nefarious.

"Why not?"

He sat down on the edge of her bed. "Starr, talk to me. I know something's going on with you."

Her chin dropped to her chest. "I got laid off."

"When?" Concern etched its way onto his face.

"About two weeks before I came home."

A look of hurt clouded Gabe's eyes. "Why didn't you say anything?"

"And be the only Lewis sibling without a job? No, thanks." She sat back down in front of her desk.

"You know Mom and Dad wouldn't care."

She snorted.

"Seriously, they wouldn't."

"Every year you guys graduated from high school and college, Dad would look at me and say 'Lewis children always excel. Remember that, Starr.'" Her heart twisted at the memory. "When I got low grades, I got a speech about remembering who I was and the importance of the family name. And the classes I *did* get high grades in weren't good enough for Dad."

"What do you mean?"

"Creative writing, literature. I excelled at the humanities, and Dad thought they were a waste of time and his money."

"Do you honestly think you're the only one who's ever been pressured to do better? Try working for him."

Starr tilted her head as she studied Gabe. A weary expression had settled over his features, dragging his normally grinning mouth into a frown. She'd been so wrapped up in her own drama and life issues that she hadn't truly thought about her brother and what he might be going through.

Lord, I'm so sorry.

She reached for Gabe's hand and squeezed it. "I'm sorry. Is it really difficult?" She always thought Gabe's comments about Dad being a taskmaster were mostly just him joking around, not showing how he really felt. Gabe loved finance. *Right?* Why had she never considered that anyone other than herself had a problem with their father's ideals?

"Of course." He loosened his tie. "I get compared to Noel all the time and reminded he will be taking over in the future. As if I was never an option."

"Then why do you work for Dad?"

"I like numbers and have a head for loans. I enjoy being able to support another person's dream." He shrugged as if to say *What else would I do?*

"Aw, you're a softie."

"Hush." His lips twisted into a wry grin.

"Do you want to run the bank?"

"No way. I just don't want Dad to shove Noel's success down my throat on a daily basis."

"I can understand that." That was one of the reasons she'd

moved to New York. A chance to strike out on her own without the constant comparisons. "You must really like your job to put up with it."

"It has its perks, and once he's retired, I won't have to listen to him anymore."

"Until you come home for family dinners."

Gabe chuckled. "Truth. Hey, change of subject. What's the latest on the wedding? I haven't seen Angel in a while."

Starr shifted in her chair. "Um, I'm not sure."

He arched an eyebrow. "Why is that exactly?"

"I, um, may have been uninvited to the wedding."

Disbelief widened Gabe's eyes. "But you're one of the maids of honor."

"Oh, brother, you're way behind on the news."

"You're not?" Gabe's mouth dropped in shock.

"I thought twins told each other everything?"

"So did I." His lips flattened as he stood. He checked his watch. "I'll call her on my way to work."

"Don't do anything on my account."

Gabe sighed. "Sum up what happened in as few words as possible."

"I asked for an apology, words were exchanged by both parties, and a decision was made for me to not go to the wedding since I'm not fond of our future brother-in-law."

"No one is." Gabe's nostrils flared. "Did she apologize?"

"What for?" She mimicked Angel's tone of voice while batting her eyelashes.

"Hmph. All right, Starr. I'll see you later."

"Later, gator."

"Love you, sis," he called over his shoulder.

A warm fuzzy feeling settled over her. She'd missed Gabe. How could she have forgotten the good times she'd had with her family? She'd been so focused on the impending doom of the wedding and coming back jobless that she'd dismissed every good memory and held on to the bad.

Lord, forgive me for wallowing in self-pity. Please help me figure out how to let go of the bad and embrace the good. She exhaled slowly. *And please help me resolve things with Angel. She's my sister, and I should remember that instead of trying to pick a fight. I don't need her to apologize in order to forgive.*

She winced. Forgiving Angel had never been high on her priority list. Sure, she'd moved on from Ashton, but her relationship with her sister had been stuck in a state of hurt and victimization. It was time to let the hurt go, even if Angel never said she was sorry.

Lord God, please soften my heart so I can truly forgive her.

She didn't want to be angry any longer. Didn't actually want to miss the wedding. If Ashton made Angel happy, then so be it. Starr would be there and congratulate them with a smile so big it would threaten to break her face.

That is, if I can undo the damage between us. Please pave the way and give me the words to reconcile our relationship. Thank You, Lord.

Her phone pinged.

Waylon
Would you like to meet up?

Starr
I'd love to. When and what are you thinking?

Waylon
Tomorrow? Zoo?

Starr
Yes! They have the ZooLights up, right?

Waylon
Yes, ma'am.

> **Starr**
> Sounds perfect.

> **Waylon**
> I'll pick you up tomorrow evening. Dress warmly.

> **Starr**
> I'll be ready.

Another day with Waylon.

She grinned. Going out on dates this Christmas had brightened Starr's holiday season. She hadn't imagined falling for her brother's best friend when she boarded the Amtrak back to DC. What would she do if David & David offered her the job back in the city? Could she stay there forever? Would their conversations wane and eventually a breakup result from the lack of communication?

Don't think about that. Focus on the fun planned for tomorrow and worry after you know if you got the job.

"Don't jump ahead, Starr Lewis."

* * * *

Starr made her way down the stairs, coat draped on her outstretched arm, just as her mother walked out of the kitchen.

Mom noted Starr's coat. "Where are you going?"

"To see the ZooLights with Waylon."

"Oh, I love that. Let me come with you."

Starr's face heated. "No. It's a date, Mom."

"He won't mind." Her mom waved a hand.

Noel came out of the living room. "What's going on?"

"I'm going with Waylon and Starr to see the ZooLights." She rushed up the stairs. "Don't leave me, Starr."

"Help," Starr whispered to her brother as her mom disappeared from sight.

"How about I go with you too?"

She squinted her eyes. Tagging along wasn't helping. Not going was the outcome she wished for.

"It's better this way," Noel explained. "I'll keep her distracted."

"Keep who distracted?" Eve asked.

Seriously, this house was like a clown car. Who else was going to pop out?

"What's going on?" Gabe asked.

Starr threw her hands up in the air. "I give up. I'm leaving."

"I'm coming," Mom yelled down the stairs.

Starr threw on her coat, grabbed her purse, and flew out the front door.

"Whoa, what's the rush?" Waylon caught her by the arms, as she neared his car.

"My mom wants to come too." She huffed out a breath. "And Noel said he would come to run interference."

"I take it you don't want a chaperone?" He grinned.

"Do we need one at the zoo? Besides, my mom and I hung out earlier today and had a great time."

"So great she doesn't want it to end." Waylon motioned with his head, and Starr turned around.

Mom led the way as Gabe, Noel, and Eve followed her out of the house.

Waylon bent down to whisper in her ear. "What do you call a date when the whole family comes?"

"Embarrassing."

He laughed.

Starr nudged him with her elbow. "Hush. Besides, I thought you wanted it to be just the two of us."

"I'm sure Noel will do as he said and give us some privacy here and there."

She poked her lip out.

"Waylon, we're going to follow you in the car," Mrs. Lewis called out as she headed for one of their Mercedes.

"Yes, ma'am."

"Who's riding with me?"

Eve raised her hand. "I will."

"Great, sweetie. Then you can drive."

Eve rolled her eyes and headed for the driver's seat.

"Guess that means me and Gabe will hitch a ride with you two." Noel's grin had a wicked bent to it.

"Way to run interference," Starr said sarcastically.

"Hey, the best place a big brother can be is right behind his little sister to make sure her *date* doesn't do anything he shouldn't." Gabe gave Waylon a mock glare.

Waylon responded with a salute, then placed his hand at the small of Starr's back. He guided her around to the passenger side and opened the door for her.

She stared up at him. "I'm so sorry."

"It's okay. We'll still be together."

Her lips upturned into a small smile. "True."

"Besides, they haven't seen you in a while. I'm sure they miss you. We'll just enjoy our time with your family." He kissed her cheek.

"All right." He'd convinced her. She wouldn't be embarrassed—*much*—and would simply take in the lights strewn about the National Zoo.

Waylon glanced in the back. "How are you guys enjoying the holiday season?"

"Haven't seen much of it besides the tree lighting ceremony," Noel remarked.

"Don't forget the constant holiday music playing at the bank," Gabe added.

"I think I've lost some brain cells as a result," Noel groused.

"Come on," Starr interjected. "You two love Christmas. Remember all the years you'd run down the hall shouting for everyone to wake up?"

"I'm pretty sure that was Gabe." Noel smirked.

"Nope." Waylon shook his head. "I remember you telling me how you guys popped off firecrackers one year to wake everyone."

Gabe laughed. "That was an epic year. I thought Mom was going to have a heart attack. She came flying out of her room holding a bat, hair in curlers."

The car filled with laughter.

"Classic." Starr wiped at her eyes. "Don't forget the year you guys stripped the tree of all the ornaments. I thought for sure Mom was going to cry when she went to snap pictures and realized the tree was bare."

"Wow. Makes me wonder what kind of antics my kids will cook up." Waylon smiled at Starr.

Her heart warmed. "How many do you want?"

Gabe groaned in the backseat. "Gross. Please don't let this conversation go where I think it's going."

"Shut up, Gabriel," Starr snapped.

Noel laughed.

Waylon caught her attention and waggled two fingers, keeping them where Gabe and Noel wouldn't see them. She smiled and nodded, mouthing, *Me too.*

The conversation flowed as they all continued to share their favorite Christmas memories, which naturally led to their favorite Christmas presents. Finally, they came up to the Connecticut Avenue entrance to the National Zoo. Waylon turned left into the parking area and followed the winding road down the hill.

"Think we'll have to park at the very bottom?" Starr asked.

"We'll see. I'm sure everyone else wants to see the lights." He stopped at the top of the hill, spotting the long line of cars. "See?"

Waylon crept behind the car in front of him until they made it to the bottom of the hill where parking lot D sat. He paid the entrance fee, and the gate lifted.

"I'm surprised Ashton and Angel couldn't make it." Waylon glanced at Starr out of the corner of his eye.

Starr considered that one of God's blessings.

"Angel said they were going to dinner with Ashton's parents," Gabe said. "She texted me to say she might come afterward."

Boo. Then again, maybe that was an opportunity for Starr to bury the hatchet.

They all exited the car and stood off to the side as they waited for Eve to park Mom's car and join them.

"I'm so glad we can all be together." Mrs. Lewis beamed as she walked over to them. "Thank you for this, Waylon. I haven't been to ZooLights in forever."

"My pleasure, Mrs. Lewis."

If anything, her grin grew bigger. "Don't you think it's about time you call me Carol?"

"Uh, thank you."

She patted his cheek, then took the lead, walking toward the entrance. On one hand, Starr was pleased her mom was being so nice. On the other hand, she was completely commandeering her date. Fortunately, Starr and Waylon ended up at the very back of the group.

"Guess Noel came through?" Waylon asked, gently taking Starr's hand.

She sighed, then peered up at him. "A huge improvement."

He smiled. "Stick with me, and you'll forget anyone else is around."

"I'm beginning to love your cheesy lines." Waylon had a way of lightening the mood and upping the attraction factor at the same time.

"That's because, secretly, your heart waits in anticipation for the next one."

Starr laughed, trying to cover up the heat blooming in her cheeks.

"And now you're laughing so you won't give it away."

"You're incorrigible." She nudged him with her elbow.

"Didn't you know a pretty smile and a nice laugh will do a guy in every time?"

"Is that right?"

"Yes, ma'am." He tucked her hand into the crook of his elbow as they started walking up the steep incline. "I have a question."

"Shoot." Starr watched him as they strolled up the hill.

"If you had a million dollars, what would you do?"

"Did I win the lottery?"

Waylon shrugged. "Or you came into some money."

"Hmm," she murmured. "I'd do what I want."

"Which is . . . ?" he drawled.

"Write," she replied softly. Since she'd been back home, she'd filled up her notebook and started on another. She couldn't remember when she had so much free time to give her hobby this much attention. She sensed sharing her deepest feelings on the subject with Waylon would be safe.

"I'd stop looking for a job and take about six months to finish my story. Polish it and see what happens. If I failed to get an agent, I wouldn't worry because I'd have the money to fall back on and probably a place to live with my parents rent free."

"Would you want to live back home?"

"Maybe while writing. I certainly wouldn't want to stay

there forever." She tilted her head. "Maybe I could offer to pay them rent money since I just won a million dollars."

"What would you write about?"

She grinned up at him. "I'd write a romance story."

"Just any romance story? Or do you already have an idea?" His steady gaze watched her, as if he cared about every word from her mouth.

"I have an idea, but I'm not ready to share yet."

"I can understand that. Thanks for sharing as much as you did."

She squeezed his arm. "What about you? What would you do with a million dollars?"

"I'm not sure."

"What about the nonprofit idea you were telling me about?" Was that no longer his dream?

"Maybe. A million dollars is certainly a good chunk of change to start a company with."

"It is."

"Only then I wonder what would happen with Mom's store."

Starr stared ahead, thinking. "Could you hire a manager to run the place for you? Then you would still own it but be able to do what you want."

"That's actually a genius idea."

Starr grinned at the contemplative look filling his face.

Waylon cleared his throat. "Getting pretty close to Angel's wedding."

"Yep." She sighed.

"Did you two make up?"

Starr shook her head. "She hasn't been around."

"You might have to go to her place."

"True." She wrinkled her nose. "I was thinking of going to the wedding anyway." She looked up at him. "What do you think?"

"You could be my plus one." Waylon winked at her.

"Crafty, Mr. Emmerson."

"More like helpful, my dear Ms. Lewis."

Starr chuckled just as they caught up to her family. She had no idea if she'd be able to make up with Angel before the wedding, but she felt the tug more and more each day to bridge the gap.

I'm listening, Lord.

✳ *fourteen* ✳

For some reason Starr was turning in circles and pumping her fist in the air, right in front of Waylon's shop.

He pushed the front door open and leaned against it. "That's an interesting dance. Care to show me the moves?"

She stilled, then slowly turned to face him. "Uh, I forgot I was in front of your shop."

"I can tell." He battled back laughter. "What are you so excited about?"

"I got a second job interview."

"A second interview? When was the first?"

Starr bit her lip as she walked into the shop. "Wednesday. The assistant just called to schedule me a second interview for Monday."

"Who with? Another PR firm?" More importantly, was it in New York?

"Yes, with David and David. My next interview will be via video, since I'm not in the area."

He froze. "It's in New York?"

"Yes."

His heart thudded as the implications took root. If she got the job, they would no longer be within fifteen miles of each other. Not that they were in an established, committed relationship or anything. They hadn't defined whatever this was. Yet the thought of her moving away made Waylon want to define it.

"If you get the job, will you move back?" He gripped the counter, waiting for her answer.

"I . . . I'd have no choice." She stepped forward. "You understand, right? I need a way to provide for myself."

"Of course." Didn't mean he liked it.

Starr stared at him. "How's your morning going?"

Really? Small talk? They never did that. "Not as good as yours." He barely resisted the urge to fold his arms and pout like a man-child. Seriously, though, his mind was reeling. He knew she was job searching. But all the times of going out and celebrating the holidays with her had pushed it far from his mind.

She grimaced. "Should I grab us something to eat at lunchtime?"

Waylon came around the counter. "Starr?"

"Yes," she whispered.

"Where are we going?" He motioned between them.

"I'm not sure."

Fair enough, but not exactly what he wanted to hear. It was time to be direct. "Do you want to be in a relationship with me?" He cupped her hands.

"I do."

Then at least they were on the same page. "How can we make this work?"

"I don't know." She bit her lip.

He stared into her eyes, trying to read the look clouding them. Was she afraid he didn't want this as much as her? *Just tell her how you feel.* He cupped her face. "I want to figure this out as well. I really like you."

"Then that means?"

"It means we'll figure this out. Together."

Her lips curved into a smile, eyes smarting with tears. "Together sounds perfect."

"Then together we'll be." He leaned down, and Starr stood on her toes to meet his kiss.

"Thank you for telling me about your interview," he said when they broke apart.

Starr nodded. "Maybe I should have done it sooner."

"Nah. We didn't declare our intentions before now."

"Our intentions?" A flirty look danced in her eyes. "As in . . . ?"

He wrapped his arms around her. "As in I'm your boyfriend, and you're my girlfriend."

"Amazing how wonderful old-fashioned words can sound."

"Better than *bae*?"

Starr giggled. "Ten times."

"I think it's my turn to share."

Her brows rose. "I'm listening."

Noel's suggestion of sharing with Starr came to mind. Waylon sighed, rubbing the back of his neck. "So I kind of have some news related to the shop." If he didn't relax, he'd break a tooth, clenching his jaw so tight.

Starr reached over and wrapped a hand around his arms. "It's okay. Whatever it is, just tell me."

"I got an offer to buy out the store. This guy called after his wife visited here, and he wants to buy it for her." He blew out a breath. "Then you made that suggestion at the zoo about hiring someone to run the place, and that sounded interesting as well." He slid his hands into his pockets. "Honestly, I don't know what to do."

Because now he kept thinking of the possibility of Starr leaving for New York. If she did, he'd hate to see her leave.

But would it be worse than saying good-bye to his mom's store?

Lord God, am I putting the cart before the horse? Starr may not even get the job.

Then again, she might. Or she could get something else in New York. Then what?

How long would either of them be willing to maintain a long-distance relationship? Sure, Waylon could take the train up to New York every other weekend, or even drive up there. Just like Starr could visit him.

What happened when their feelings ran deeper? If Waylon kept his shop and Starr maintained a job in NYC, something had to give. *Can I give up the shop?*

"What was your gut reaction when he made the offer?" Starr asked.

"To imagine what I could do with a million dollars."

Her jaw dropped. "Is he really offering a million?"

"A little over."

"Oh wow. No wonder you had the hypothetical question." She tilted her head. "Does our relationship factor in to your decision?"

"It definitely does now that we said we want to make us work." Which still made him want to grin and throw a fist in the air in jubilation.

How far could a million dollars go in NYC?

"Do you want to run your mom's store?"

His heart squeezed. "I don't know. Since you've helped me spruce it up " He paused. "That was not a Christmas tree joke."

She laughed. "Good."

"Since the name change and miniature facelift the shop got, foot traffic has increased. I'm not sure yet if the momentum will carry past the season, but my initial fears have waned.

I've also enjoyed talking to the customers and helping them find the perfect ornaments."

Even Mrs. Blackwell had brought cheer with her.

"But I like the idea of my nonprofit as well. Now my mind is also wondering if you will be in New York. If so, maybe I should sell the store, and—"

"Waylon." Starr held up her hands. "Sorry, trying to pump the brakes on that thought, but at the same time, trying not to freak out over the pressure. We don't even know if we'll fall for each other. You know, say those three little words."

"When I say them, they won't have a little impact."

Her cheeks flushed. "You know what I mean."

"Yes, but I couldn't resist teasing."

"You don't think this is too much pressure for an early relationship?"

He sighed. "I mean, yes. But my mind keeps asking what-if. What if you're the one? What if what we have is just the beginning of a fantastic life together? I don't want to miss it because I should have sold my mom's shop and followed you to New York." And now that the words were out there, he realized it was true.

"I don't want you to follow me to NYC and sell your mom's store if I was supposed to look for a job in DC and support your work here." She shifted on her feet. "Have you been praying about the offer?"

"Yes."

"Good." She smiled. "Then I'll add my prayers to yours. We need to pray that we don't let jobs impact our relationship and stress us out as we're getting to know each other in a different way. We'll simply pray that we know what to do about who lives where."

He placed his forehead against hers. "Okay. But please know I would never resent you if I believed selling was the best thing."

"So you know, I've been praying about DC since you brought it up."

Happiness flooded his heart. "Have you really?"

She nodded.

"Thank you."

"Of course. I want to be where you are."

He groaned. "You say the best things. Maybe you should be saying the one-liners."

She laughed. "How about we both do?"

"Sounds like a plan."

Now for them to figure out where to live and what to do about their jobs.

❄ *fifteen* ❄

Lord, please be with me.

Starr said amen and opened her eyes. On a long exhale, she knocked on Angel's door. This morning she'd woken with the pressing need to resolve their differences before Angel's wedding, which was in two days. They were sisters, and Starr didn't want a man to come between them.

Yet with every passing second, doubt plagued her. Had Angel looked through the peephole and seen Starr and made the choice not to let her in? Gabe had verified that Angel would be home today at this time. Surely his twin radar—or most likely a text—hadn't been incorrect. She lifted her hand to knock again, but the door flew open.

"Oh, it's you."

"Hi." Starr spoke softly, hoping her tone would convey she wasn't here for a fight.

"What do you want?" Angel folded her arms.

"Could I come in so we can talk?"

"Why would you want to talk to me?"

Lord, please help me not lose my temper. "Because you're my sister, Angel."

Her big sister's lips flattened. After a moment, Angel moved to the side to let Starr past.

She kept her hands in her pockets, gripping the insides like a lifeline. "How have you been?"

"Small talk, Starr?"

"Please, just let me . . ." She blew out a breath. *Lord, please soften Angel's heart.* The whispered prayer had been repeating in Starr's mind all this morning, especially when Starr had sat in the pew at church and noted Angel's absence. "I'm sorry."

Angel's eyes widened. "What did you say?"

"I'm sorry." Starr took a step forward. "I should've never made you feel like I didn't want to support you or celebrate your wedding. Of course I want to come and see you get married. You're the first of us to do so, and we're sisters." She finished the last part in a low voice, the energy from her speech already draining her.

"Then you're not jealous?" Skepticism coated every word.

"No!" Starr took a calming breath. "No. I'm happy for you."

Angel genuinely seemed happy to be marrying Ashton. As much as Starr thought he made a horrible boyfriend and fiancé, Angel loved him, and that had to count for something. So Starr would support her and remind herself the wedding wasn't about what happened with Ashton.

A tear slid down Angel's cheek.

Starr's breath hitched. Would Angel forgive her?

Suddenly, her sister rushed toward Starr. Angel wrapped her arms around Starr's waist in a death grip, while sobbing into the side of her neck.

Oh my goodness. Not the response she'd anticipated. She hugged her sister, rubbing soothing circles on Angel's back. "Why are you crying?"

"He didn't want me!"

"What?" *What in the world is going on?*

147

Starr led them to the couch and helped Angel sit, then angled toward her sister, their knees almost touching. Starr pulled some tissues from her purse and passed one to Angel. She'd packed them in preparation for tears, but never in a million years had she pictured this kind of scenario.

"Tell me what's going on."

Angel dabbed at her eyes. "I overheard Ashton talking to his dad when we went over for dinner."

"Right. Gabe told us where you were."

"I heard his father congratulating him on the upcoming nuptials. And he told his father"—she sniffled—"'Like you said, Dad, "Marry a girl who'll make you look good to your boss." That's Angel in a nutshell.'"

Starr reared back. That slimy . . . *Breathe, Starr.* "Then what happened?"

"I listened a little more. Apparently, Ashton only wanted to marry me because he thought I would make the perfect arm candy for his political career."

Starr winced inwardly. What did that say about *her*? *It's not about you. Listen to Angel.*

"He also liked that I come from money."

"Oh, honey." Starr ran a hand down Angel's back.

"I was so furious I called off the wedding." Angel wiped at the tears, leaving black trails in their wake.

"Are you serious?"

Her sister nodded.

Starr's heart thumped as she searched for the right words. "Did you tell Mom?"

"No," Angel choked out. "I feel like such a fool. I don't know what to do," she wailed.

"Please, don't say that." She squeezed Angel's hand and rubbed her back with the other. "Ashton is the one who's in the wrong."

"I thought we were soul mates. I've never had a man say such sweet things to me. Everything he said made me fall deeper and deeper in love." Angel clutched her heart as if it pained her . . . or was breaking. "How am I going to get through this, Starr?"

"Oh, Angel," she whispered, wrapping her sister in a hug. "I'll be here. We'll all be here for you."

"How can I tell everyone the wedding's off?"

"You won't. Eve and I can take care of that. I'm sure Mom will want to help as well."

Angel pulled back, disbelief widening her eyes. "I can't believe you would do that for me."

"Why wouldn't I?" That's what sisters were for.

"I treated you so horribly." More tears spilled down her cheeks.

Starr blew out a breath. "Like I keep telling you, we're sisters. I love you, and I've already forgiven you." She woke up this morning, saying those exact words to the Lord. And for the first time, she'd meant them. It was why she had the courage to face her sister now and mend the rift.

God had answered Starr's prayers and brought her healing.

"I don't deserve forgiveness."

"None of us ever do."

"Thank you, sister." Angel leaned her head on Starr's shoulder, and they sat that way until Angel's tears finally stopped.

* * * *

Starr set her phone down on her bedroom desk. David & David wanted to hire her. She'd been shocked when they'd offered the job right after the questions ended for her video interview.

So why wasn't she happy? Where were the feelings of elation and relief?

Instead, her stomach gurgled as her stress mounted. Though the offer included everything Starr could possibly want, it no longer held the same appeal it would have had she not committed to a relationship with Waylon. She'd be accepting the job out of a desire for security, not because it was her dream. She couldn't even claim she liked working in public relations the way Gabe liked working in finance. If he could like numbers enough to put up with Dad, shouldn't she feel the same way about her work?

Why did she want to return to New York when she'd been happier here than she'd ever been there?

Lord, what do I do? A week ago, I would have jumped at the opportunity. Yet after dating Waylon and daydreaming about his million-dollar question, I'm wishing for things I don't have. What's the right decision here?

David & David expected a response to their offer letter the day after Christmas. Her stomach burned with indecision. Should she accept the position and endure a long-distance relationship with Waylon? If they didn't work out, at least she'd have a job. But what if they did work out? Would Waylon sell his shop and move to New York? Or should Starr risk turning down a bona fide offer and look for a job in DC instead? She placed her palm to her forehead. So many questions, so many scenarios. Most importantly, she had to make the decision God wanted her to. *You won't do that if you're imagining everything that can go wrong. Relax, let God direct you.*

Starr stood, sliding her phone into her back jean pocket as she walked down the stairs and headed for the kitchen. Voices reached her ears as she headed down the hall. Sounded like her mom and Angel were talking. Angel had stayed over last night after falling into their mother's arms and crying all over again.

Mom had been indignant regarding Ashton's duplicity. She'd kindly offered to make all the calls necessary to stop the wedding. Starr wondered what the extended family had thought after receiving those calls. Surely they had already made their travel arrangements. Starr knew Gabe and Noel had been itching for a fight, which she and Eve had been able to talk them out of.

She stepped into the kitchen. Mom smiled and motioned her over. She walked to where they sat at the island.

Mom enveloped Starr. "Thank you for being there for your sister yesterday," she whispered.

"It was nothing."

Mom pulled back and smoothed Starr's hair away from her face. "It was something."

She nodded, feeling tears brimming.

"I'm proud of you."

Starr's bottom lip trembled. Why? Starr had been keeping her job situation a secret. She shouldn't be applauded for being there for her sister. Who wouldn't?

"Uh-oh. What's wrong?" Mom asked.

Starr straightened. "Nothing." She wouldn't bring up her situation and detract from what Angel was going through.

"Are you sure? You have that look you get when something's bothering you."

"Worry about Angel, Mom." She sidestepped her and headed for the cookie jar. "Do you still have some Grinch cookies?" The green sugar cookies were the best. Her mom always added red M&M's to the batter as well.

"Noel ate them all."

"Drat." She frowned, tapping her fingers on the countertop.

"I frosted some other sugar cookies last night." Her mom

151

pointed to some plastic containers as she took a seat on a barstool next to Angel.

"Are they for someone else?" Her mom usually stored cookies in the cookie jar.

"Your father is taking some to work tomorrow. But I have to bake more, so feel free to take from one of those containers."

Starr opened the top one and laughed. "Looks like someone beat me to it." A row of cookies was missing.

"That was me." Angel shrugged. "Comfort food."

Her mom patted Angel on the hand. "Will you be staying for dinner?"

"No." Angel stood. "I should go back to my place and try to figure out what to do now."

"How about tomorrow we do something fun?"

"I don't know, Mom," Angel said.

"Yes, sweetie. You need to think about something else. How about I get tickets to Handel's *Messiah* at the National Cathedral?" Mom clasped her hands in a pleading motion.

"All right."

Starr's heart ached at the somber expression on Angel's face. She hated how things had turned out for her. *Lord, please help her heal.*

"You won't regret it, Angel. Family time is just what you need."

"Okay, Mom. Bye, Starr."

Starr waved to Angel, then sat on the vacated barstool and bit into a sugar cookie, doing a happy dance when the frosting hit her tongue. So good.

"Now that Angel's gone, you wanna tell me what's really bothering you?"

Starr sputtered, bits of cookie flying everywhere as they attempted to travel down the wrong pipe. Her mom handed her a glass of water and patted her on the back.

"I'm fine. You can stop," she choked out. If her mom beat her back one more time, she'd break a rib.

"What's going on with you, Starr?"

She set her cookie down and met her mom's gaze. "I got laid off."

Mom's mouth fell open. "When?"

"Before I came here." She could feel a sheepish expression creeping onto her face and heating her cheeks.

"Why didn't you say anything?"

Yikes. Mom's voice had reached a frequency that would attract the neighborhood dogs.

"I was embarrassed." *Still am.*

"Oh, Starr. There was no reason to be. You know you always have a place here."

She bit her lip. "Do you really mean that?"

"Yes, baby." Her mother framed her face with warm hands. "You're my daughter. My baby. You have to know I would do anything in my power to help you if needed."

Starr's eyes watered. "What if I wanted to hang around for a few months and work on a novel?" She held her breath, searching her mom's warm brown eyes.

"Is that what you want? To write a novel?"

"Yes." Her voice came out clear and confident.

If God would somehow make a way for her to turn her dreams into reality, she would write for real and not claim it to be a mere hobby. Writing had always been her dream, but also something she believed to be unattainable. Only now the question was, What if it was actually within reach? What if fear had been the only thing holding her back?

"If you really want to, then yes. You can stay here and write your novel." Her mom dropped her hands and grabbed one of the cookies. "What would you write about?"

"Love. Acceptance. Faith over fear." It's what she'd been

writing in her notebook since she came home, and Waylon gave her the courage to continue writing.

It's why she'd been contemplating transferring it from paper to laptop.

Her mom smiled. "That sounds wonderful. I can't wait to read it."

Starr let out a breath. *Thank You for direction.* If she could stay here and not worry about having a roof over her head and food in her stomach, then Starr would spend time writing the story she was beginning to realize God had put in her heart.

Thank You for this opportunity to make my dream a reality. Lord, I turn over this love of writing to You. For You to do with it as You will. Whether I can be published or if it is just meant for me to accomplish finishing a novel, may I honor You regardless of the outcome. Amen.

❆ sixteen ❆

The shop was quiet. All patrons had left for the day, and the *Closed* sign had been flipped over for at least ten minutes. Waylon pulled down the ornaments he kept on the top shelf for safekeeping. His apartment really didn't have the necessary storage space, so he'd snuck his prized possessions into the shop.

He opened the lid and smiled. The bin was filled with family ornaments made by him, Joanna, and their mom. From the time he'd been old enough to help, they'd made ornaments together every year. This year, he'd been too sad to hang them on the Christmas tree in his apartment. He'd been thinking about turning them over to Joanna despite her insistence that he keep them. Now he was thankful he hadn't, because parting with them felt like losing a piece of his mom all over again.

The ornaments held sentimental value just like this shop. Being able to chat with customers who knew his mom and were blessed by her presence brightened his day. Remembering which songs were her favorites and made her want to dance put a smile on his face. The memories weren't painful like they were when he sat in his apartment all alone.

The changes Starr helped him implement had put him in the

155

black. Now that the fear of losing money had receded, coming to the shop was fun. The place was almost like a second home.

In his prayers, he'd asked God to show him why he should keep the shop, *if* that was the right thing to do. The memories kept alive in the four walls were a huge reason to keep running the store. Obviously, his mom left him the shop for a reason. He always wanted to honor that, but now his sense of obligation had fled. The overwhelming love he had for his mom had transformed how he viewed the shop. It was no longer obedience to his mom's will but a heart for the people who walked in the door.

As much as the money Mr. Blackwell was offering appealed, riches wouldn't connect him to his mother. Therefore, Waylon couldn't part with her shop—*his* shop. Hopefully any future Emmersons would be happy to run the place and create lasting memories of their time together.

Rightness settled in his chest as the peace of his decision filled him. Waylon picked up his cell and dialed Mr. Blackwell. God willing, the gentleman would understand.

"Mr. Emmerson, I wondered when you'd call."

"Sorry for the delay, sir."

"No problem at all. Tell me you've signed the papers."

Waylon winced. "Actually, sir, I'm calling to decline your generous offer."

"Is it too low?"

Did that mean he'd go higher? Waylon shook his head. "No, sir. This shop used to be my mother's, and she passed six months ago. I don't want to part with it."

"I'm sorry for your loss. I can understand keeping something like that in the family."

Waylon cleared his throat. "Sir, I do have a counteroffer. I was wondering if maybe your wife would like to work here? I know it's not ownership, but perhaps she'd enjoy herself." He wouldn't mind the help, and if Starr left DC, maybe he could, too, if he had a good manager.

"Hey, now you're putting money in my pocket. It's a sound offer. I'll talk to her about it."

"Good. She can stop by after Christmas if she's interested."

"I'll let her know."

"Merry Christmas, Mr. Blackwell."

"Same to you, Mr. Emmerson."

Waylon sighed with relief and leaned back into his chair. That was the right decision. All he had to do now was to wait and see what God had planned for Waylon's relationship with Starr. If they were meant to have a life together, he'd trust God to work out all the details.

* * * *

Waylon tilted his head back and stood in awe of the National Cathedral. The creators of the cathedral were nothing short of masterful in their architecture. The pinnacles and flying buttresses—key identifiers of Gothic architecture—immediately caught the eye, but what made the view so spectacular today was the added dusting of snow that had begun to fall. The surrounding trees glittered, making the scene look like something out of a movie.

People passed by, completely ignoring the scene before them. How could they not stop and stare? At least he had the time to stop and smell the roses. Of course, he was meeting up with Starr and her family, so gawking at the church seemed in line with the order of business. Perhaps he'd come back another day for one of the tours and simply soak up the atmosphere.

Waylon pulled out his phone to see if Starr had texted him her location yet. Maybe the Lewis family had beaten him here, considering how close by they lived.

"Waylon!"

He turned and smiled. Starr waved at him from the midst of her family. His eyes flitted to Angel, who wore a downcast expression. When Starr told him the wedding was off, he'd been shocked. At the same time, a little relieved. He still thought about that little surprise visit from Ashton. Angel probably wouldn't appreciate hearing about it, but Waylon was glad she hadn't married someone so conniving and two-faced.

Starr broke away from the group and smiled at him, snow-flakes making her eyelashes sparkle. "Hey, you."

"Isn't that supposed to be my line?" He took her gloved hand in his.

"I'm sure you have a much more impressive one to feed me."

Waylon stopped and took off his gloves. "Hold these, please."

"But it's freezing out here."

"Nah, you're so hot I don't need them."

Starr groaned, her head dropping forward.

Waylon let out a chuckle as her shoulders shook with laughter.

"I can't believe I fell for that."

"It's a good thing you did. It would have been embarrassing on my end had you not." He slid his gloves back on as they followed her family down the sidewalk. He leaned down. "How's Angel?"

Starr's eyes flickered toward her sister, then back to him. "She finally stopped crying. Not sure if that's a good thing or not."

"I'll be praying for her."

"Thank you. I'm sure she'd appreciate it."

It was nice of the family to find a last-minute activity to attend so that Angel didn't have to think about the wedding that wasn't. Though Waylon suspected she'd think about it regardless.

They walked inside, and he tugged his scarf loose, then stuffed his gloves into his coat pockets. Ushers guided them toward the seating area. The orchestra members were slowly setting up. Some practiced scales while others flipped through the sheet music on the stands.

"Is this the extended version or the family-friendly one?" He knew from the cathedral's website that they offered a shorter version in case people wanted to bring their young children.

"I'm not sure."

Waylon sat back and put an arm around Starr. She snuggled into his side, and warmth filled his insides. He could happily sit next to this woman for the rest of his life.

Not that he was ready for *that* level of commitment. They weren't that far into their relationship, but it was something his brain had been turning to more and more. What would life look like if Starr was his wife?

He squeezed her shoulders, placing a kiss on her forehead.

"Are you coming over after the concert?" she asked softly.

"I would like to."

"Then come. I missed you today." Her cheeks bloomed as if she was embarrassed to admit that aloud.

"Same here." His mind had strayed to her more times than he could count. Plus, he had news to share with her.

"Then it's a date."

"With lots of chaperones."

She chuckled. "You'll survive."

"We'll see, huh?"

He clamped his lips shut as the conductor walked onto the stage. The man thanked everyone for coming and explained the beauty of the Christmas season and the power of Jesus's birth. Waylon slowly tuned him out as he thought of his Lord and Savior.

Lord God, thank You for sending Your Son to us. I can't even imagine how it must have felt to know He would be crucified. But You loved us so much, You were willing to make that sacrifice. Thank You for giving us a way back to You. Thank You for forgiving me for my sins, those of the past, present, and yet to come.

He winced. Hopefully those would be minimal. It stung to admit he would sin again, knowing the change he'd already experienced when he first accepted Christ as his Savior. Yet it was also a relief knowing God would be willing to forgive if Waylon repented.

Thank You for this Christmas season. I was worried I would be a mess without my mom or Joanna to see me through. But You provided companionship in the Lewis family. And Starr. Lord, I pray that You have a future mapped out for us that will last until I draw my final breath.

Because even if he wasn't ready to say the *L* word or propose, he knew she was the one. Felt the truth in every fiber of his being.

He couldn't wait to make his first Christmas memory with Starr. He leaned over to whisper in her ear. "Should we exchange gifts at your parents' place?"

She arched an eyebrow. "Aren't you coming over tomorrow?"

"Yeah, but if we exchange gifts today, we can do it privately."

"I'd like that."

He kissed her forehead. "Then it's a plan."

* * * *

Waylon sat with Starr on the couch in the Lewises' den. Noel and Gabe were somewhere in the house hanging out

160

with Mr. Lewis. Mrs. Lewis, Eve, and Angel were baking for tomorrow. Thanks to Mrs. Lewis's timely departure from the den, he and Starr were alone, nestled in the back of the house ready to exchange gifts.

"I have to tell you something first," Starr said, placing her chin on her hand. "I'm not going back to New York."

His pulse raced. "Did you not get the job?" Did his tone sound appropriately sad for her, while carefully hiding the elation that she would stay in DC?

"Actually, I sent them an email last night explaining that I was withdrawing my application." She stared into his eyes. "There are people I want to be near and a dream I want to pursue."

"Does that mean you'll be writing?"

She smiled. "It does. I started transferring the story in my notebook to my laptop yesterday."

He enveloped her in his arms. "I'm so happy for you. And for me." He pulled back. "I know your story's going to be amazing."

"How? What if I stink as a writer?"

"If you're still at the same level as your high school story, then you'll be great. If you've improved, I know success is at your fingertips."

Starr stared at him for a few heartbeats. "Why do you believe in me so much?"

"How can I not? You're great at everything you try." He tucked a strand of her hair behind her ear. "I also came to a decision about the store."

She leaned forward. "What did you decide?"

"To keep it. It's not just my mom's anymore. I want to work there and keep it for any future kids I may have." He shrugged. "Or give it to Joanna's kids if my kids aren't interested."

"I was hoping you'd keep it! Even when I thought going

back to New York was the right thing, I wanted you to keep the store."

"Looks like we made decisions right for us and right for us as a couple."

She grinned. "Isn't that beautiful how it worked?"

"Very beautiful." He closed the distance between them and kissed her softly on the lips. "Present time."

She giggled. "Okay. Let me give you my present first."

Waylon took the proffered gift. He popped the lid of the box and stared at the beaded bracelets resting inside.

"So you may be wondering why two bracelets. It's simple. One is for you, one is for me." Starr cleared her throat. "I, uh, I know we haven't been dating that long, so I wanted something meaningful but lighthearted."

Waylon took out the black beaded bracelet. "Is this one mine?"

Starr nodded. She took out the purple one and placed it on her wrist. "Now you put yours on."

"Okay." He really didn't wear jewelry. Waylon wasn't sure how he felt about a bracelet, even though the black beads were on the masculine side. "Why bracelets?"

"Hold up your arm."

He did, and when she put hers next to his, they stuck together. "What in the world?"

She grinned. "Magnetic couple bracelets. Now you know I'll be stuck to you like glue."

"Oh man. This is so cheesy." He kissed her right cheek. "So perfect." He kissed her left cheek. "Thank you."

"You're welcome."

He reached for the gift bag he'd put her present in. Starr pulled out the red and green tissue paper.

"Candles? I love candles." She pulled out the first one, read the label, then her head fell back as laughter bubbled from her.

"Which one is that?"

"*First draft.*"

"And what does it smell like?"

"'Desperation, hope, and two-day old coffee,'" she said, amusement coating every word.

"I thought they would inspire you whenever you wrote."

"And you picked these before you knew I was going to stay and write?"

"I hoped that even if you left for New York, you'd still choose to write."

"What do the others say?" She pulled out the second jar. "This one is *editing*. And it smells like 'indecision, worry, and red ink.'"

"I think that one is my favorite."

Starr shook her head. "No. I think *published author* will be mine."

"I don't remember those smells."

"'Victory, new book, and what next.'" Her face beamed with joy. "These are great. Thank you so much." She threw her arms around him.

"My pleasure." He tucked his nose into the dip of her neck. "Thank you for making this season bearable."

"Likewise. This has been one of my best Christmases yet." Starr kissed him. "Now to survive dinner tomorrow with the whole gang."

"We got this."

❄ seventeen ❄

A foghorn ripped Starr from her dream. She shot up in bed, trying to orient herself. Had that noise been in her dream?

Brrrr!

She winced. Ugh. Probably one of her childish brothers running up and down the halls with a horn. All the Lewis siblings had gone to their old rooms after hanging out at the cathedral the day before. Angel hadn't wanted to be alone on her almost wedding day, and none of Starr's other siblings had wanted to drive in the snow that refused to stop falling.

Her lips pursed. Come to think of it, the snow had been bad when Waylon left. Did that mean he wouldn't be able to come over for Christmas dinner today? Unless the city had plowed early, Waylon would have no way to navigate the roads. The DC metro area reacted strangely to snowfall. Every year white precipitation fell from the skies, and every year the city waffled over whether they should or should not plow the streets. Sometimes the transportation did an awesome job, and other times, one had to slip and slide down the streets.

Starr removed her silk headwrap and took a brush to her light brown hair. After throwing on a sweater and jeans, she slid her feet into some fur ankle boots and trudged her way out of the room. She'd already placed the presents that Waylon had helped her pick out for her family under the tree last night.

She smiled thinking of the gifts they'd exchanged yesterday. His were so thoughtful. She'd have to light one of the candles when she worked on her manuscript again.

Gabe spotted her and stopped running, a wide grin on his face and a foghorn in his hand. "Merry Christmas, Starr."

"Merry Christmas." She gave him a side hug. "And thanks for the wake-up call." She rolled her eyes.

He pressed the horn, and she jumped. "My pleasure."

"You're such a pain!" She shoved him, and he laughed all the way to his room.

Noel followed close behind him. "I told him not to do it."

"Sure you did. You probably have one behind your back."

He winked and another foghorn blared loudly.

She pressed a hand to her heart and hurried away. No way did she want to hear that sound again.

"Starr, is that you?" her mom called from the kitchen.

Starr held out her hands in a ta-da motion. "Merry Christmas." She walked over to Mom and kissed her on the cheek. "It smells good in here."

"Thank the Lord I was already up when your foolish brothers tried to wake the dead."

"Oh, they did. That first blast stopped my heart, and the next one jump-started it again."

Her mom chuckled. "I'm sure your sisters didn't appreciate it either. Can you set the dining table for me?"

"Sure." Starr inhaled the wonderful aroma of cinnamon rolls that filled the kitchen. "Are they getting ready?"

"Most likely. Your brothers certainly made sure they aren't still sleeping."

Truth. Starr grabbed the Christmas plates from the pantry.

"Hopefully Waylon heard the blast and is getting ready for breakfast as well."

"Wait. What?" She whirled around and tensed as she heard one of the plates start to slide. She halted its projection.

"I let him stay in the guest room. We couldn't send him out in those conditions."

Starr's heart pounded, and she stared down at her clothes. She would have chosen a dress had she known. "Oh."

Her mother snickered. "Relax, sweetie. You look beautiful."

Starr's cheeks warmed, and she hustled out of the kitchen. Trust her mom to read her mind about whether or not she looked Christmas worthy for her new boyfriend.

She entered the dining room and immediately began placing a decorative plate onto each mat in front of the chairs. Mom had already put out a few miniature trees in the middle of the table as centerpieces. Starr went back to the kitchen to grab silverware and napkins, then headed back to the dining area.

As she rolled up the napkins and placed a holly-berry napkin ring around them, someone made a coughing noise. She looked up to see Waylon standing in the doorway, a bemused expression on his face.

"Merry Christmas." He smiled warmly.

"Merry Christmas to you too. I didn't know you stayed over." She eyed the plaid shirt he must have borrowed from Gabe. Noel only owned dress shirts, so it couldn't be his. "Looking very dapper."

Waylon held the plaid away from his chest. "Gabe said it would make me look festive."

Starr grinned. "It does." She placed a hand on her hip. "What happened last night? I know we kissed good night and you headed outside."

"That we did." He winked. "But when I went to get in the car, I realized I needed the shovel from my trunk. After watch-

166

ing me make a futile attempt to compete with the still-falling snow, your mom invited me to stay over."

"It was really that much?" Not that she looked all that hard when Waylon had left. A breeze had sliced right through her outfit last night and sent her running for warmth.

"I probably could've made it home, but she made it easy for me not to have to worry about driving in the snow."

Starr placed the last napkin down and walked toward him. Waylon opened his arms, and she stepped right into them, resting her head on his chest. She sighed in contentment as his heart beat steadily under her ear.

"What a perfect Christmas Day," she mumbled against his chest.

His arms tightened. "I agree."

"Ugh. Not on Christmas," Noel groused as he entered the room.

Starr stepped back and grinned cheekily at her brother. "One day you will have a woman who makes you smile more than spreadsheets and ledgers."

Gabe snorted. "Not likely."

"I could have a girlfriend. I just choose not to." Noel arched a brow.

"Sure you do." Eve shook her head at Noel.

"Who's going to bring these dishes out here?" Mom asked the full room.

They all filtered into the kitchen, grabbing a breakfast dish at Mom's insistence. As they finally took their places around the dining table, Starr looked around the room and thought about how different today was compared to when she first got off the train at Union Station.

She'd come home begrudgingly and as a last resort. Yet hanging out with her family and doing Christmas activities had thawed her hurt feelings of being the youngest and the only one without a successful career. It also gave her a new perspective. She saw how Noel worked himself too hard. How Gabe was miserable listening to their dad compare him to Noel. How Eve had to remodel after the flood. Not to mention she focused too much on work and left no time for fun. Her siblings' lives were not as perfect as Starr had thought.

But what made the hardships easier to bear was when they gathered together as a family. Like how they protected Angel from the backlash of a last-minute wedding cancellation on Christmas Eve. Together they had fun, made memories, and made sure no one was left alone. Viewing her family through the eyes of adulthood and her own growth made Starr so glad she had returned home.

With the added bonus of falling for Waylon, this had been the best Christmas of her life. He'd made every day they were together fun. He was the embodiment of the Christmas spirit with his cheesy jokes, kindness, and willingness to honor his mom even after death.

Starr had been so sure coming back home would be nothing but disappointment. Instead, it was the best thing she could've ever done.

"Merry Christmas!" Mom yelled.

"Merry Christmas!" they all chorused.

❄ *epilogue* ❄

MAY

"It's here!" Starr held up the manila envelope as she made her way toward Waylon.

Fortunately, Mrs. Blackwell was helping a customer, which left Waylon free to listen to her news. The store had been decorated in red, white, and blue to market ornaments and decorations reminiscent of Independence Day. Granted, they had another two months before July rolled around, but people liked to shop early. Plus, Starr knew he had plans for a Christmas-in-July event.

"Did you open the envelope already?"

"No. I wanted to share the news with you."

He kissed her cheek. "I love you."

"I love you too." Her heart still swooned whenever they declared their feelings.

Waylon had been the first to say *I love you* back in March when he took her on a picnic. She'd quickly returned the sentiment and had been relieved to know the feeling was mutual.

"Go on, open it."

169

"Right." She slid a finger at the envelope's edge and ripped it open. Then Starr pulled out her publishing contract.

It's real.

She was actually going to become a published author. Well, in eighteen months from signing the contract when her book hit bookstores. Starr had finished her first draft in three months and secured an agent shortly after that. Her agent said she must be a natural to finish a draft that quickly, but she chalked that up to having no job and copious amounts of alone time. She really had no choice *but* to write.

Yet never in a million years had she imagined getting a contract so quickly.

"It's beautiful," she whispered.

Waylon's deep chuckle shot a thrill through her. "You're beautiful, Ms. Future Published Author. I bought something just for this occasion."

He handed her a small, rectangular box. Starr smiled up at him. "Thank you."

She untied the light blue ribbon and removed the lid. Inside lay a velvet box, which she quickly opened. A black pen with her name etched in silver shined back at her.

"Waylon!" she gasped.

"I figured you'd need a pen to sign all the contracts you'll be getting."

She slid an arm around him. "Thank you so much."

"My pleasure. Now sign the papers so I can take pictures for you to post on your social media accounts."

Starr posed with the pen above the signature block and smiled.

After Waylon took a few shots, he put his cell down. "I have one more present for you." The twinkle in his eyes had Starr grinning.

"Another one?" Her heart practically melted at the sound of his laughter. "Is it another writing gift?"

"Nope."

This time he handed her a square box. Too big to be a ring box. Disappointment filtered through her, but she pushed it back. There was no rush. He'd propose when the time was right.

But, Lord, let it be sometime soon, please.

Starr pulled at the end of the ribbon, unraveling the bow. Lifting the lid, she sighed with pleasure. "A glass ornament."

She lifted the fuchsia orb from the box and squinted. Cursive writing had been etched on the outside. She stilled the ornament with her other hand to get a better look.

Waylon and Starr. May 20th until forever.

Her breath caught. Slowly, Starr turned toward Waylon to find him on one knee with an open ring box.

"Starr Lewis, you make me thankful for every single day I have with you. I cannot wait to see what life holds for us. Will you marry me?"

"Yes! All the yeses."

His lips curved into the smile she loved so much as he stood, wrapping her up in his strong arms.

A deep chuckle reverberated through her as she rested her head against his chest. He squeezed her close, then pulled back. "Let me see your ring finger."

Starr held out a shaky hand and watched as a diamond solitaire slid onto her finger. "It's gorgeous," she murmured.

"Just like you."

"Ah, there's your cheesy line."

acknowledgments

I never thought I'd be able to write an acknowledgment page twice. So if you've read this story before (previously titled *I'll Be Home*), then this may look familiar. However, you'll see some new additions.

First, thank you to Bethany House for giving this story new life. I was over-the-moon excited when you guys planned to republish this story. Thank you to Jessica Sharpe, Kate Deppe, and all the others at Bethany House who contributed to the publication. I appreciate all of you!

Thank you to my agent, Rachel McMillan. I still pinch myself that I get to call you my agent. I'm so glad you're in my corner and helping me in this writing journey. You're the best!

Thank you to my readers for helping me come up with names for Waylon's Christmas shop. You'll notice I used some of your suggestions in the brainstorming scene he had with Starr. I so appreciate you!

I also have to thank the best critique partners a girl could ask for. Andrea Boyd, Jaycee Weaver, and Sarah Monzon, I couldn't have finished this book without you. Your feedback is as invaluable as your friendship.

Last, I'd like to thank my husband and boys. Giving me time to write is such a precious gift, especially when it takes time away from you. Thank you for being my champions and putting up with Christmas music out of season. I love you.

For more from
TONI SHILOH,
read on for an excerpt from

the

LOVE
SCRIPT

Hollywood hair stylist and makeup artist Neveah loves making those in the spotlight look their best. But when the spotlight is on her after a photo of her and Hollywood heartthrob Lamont goes viral for all the wrong reasons, they suddenly find themselves in a fake relationship to save their careers. In a world where nothing seems real, can Neveah be true to herself . . . and her heart?

AVAILABLE NOW
wherever books are sold.

One

The wind whipped through the car's sunroof, the sound competing with a serenade by H.E.R. on the R&B station as I drove down Coldwater Canyon. Privacy hedges created lush scenery against the clear sky peeking through the trees. Today's weather reminded me of the Southern California often portrayed in movies—abundant sunshine, not too hot and not too cold. The perfect temps made traveling across metro Los Angeles a dream.

My next client appointment was with Ms. Rosie Booker, one of the sweetest women I'd ever met. She'd overcome breast cancer while keeping her eyes on God, making her my hero and an inspiration all in one. As her personal hair stylist, I'd had the honor of keeping her hair healthy as it grew back into its former glory. She always imparted wisdom throughout our sessions, leaving me encouraged and ready to face whatever came my way. Working with her in the comfort of her home was a lot different from when I worked on set as a film hair stylist. Unfortunately, my last position working on a streaming show was about six months ago.

I'd been applying for more jobs in the film industry, but the rejections had me hustling to book freelance positions as a personal stylist and showing up to my part-time salon position at The Mane Do. Maybe one day I'd be able to tack on *key hair stylist* next to my name, Nevaeh Richards. Be the one who turned a normal actor into the next Carrie Fisher, known for her iconic hairstyles in the *Star Wars* franchise. Or maybe I could even be a part of the next blockbuster movie that had fierce warriors like the Dora Milaje in *Black Panther*. And I certainly wouldn't sneeze at an Academy Award win either.

I'd actually stumbled onto the job with Ms. Rosie. Lamont Booker—yes, *the* Sexiest Man Alive (SMA)—had been one of the actors on a Netflix show I'd worked on set with last year. Back then his mother, Ms. Rosie, had just shaved her head to combat the copious amounts of hair loss from chemo treatments. Lamont Booker overheard me talking about wigs, hair care, and the importance of a skin-care regime to one of the supporting actresses. Shortly after, he'd offered me the position of his mother's personal hair stylist. Now I came by their place once a week to style her curly tresses and pamper her as the locks grew back in. I didn't know a lot about the Sexiest Man Alive, but he sure did love his mom. Then again, she was an easy person to love.

The road curved, and I grinned as Lamont Booker's multimillion-dollar home came into view. The white structure gleamed in the California sunlight, the black trim adding a masculine touch. Though Lamont Booker—sorry, I can only say and think both his first and last names—lived with his mother. Well, *he* didn't live with his mother. He'd insisted Ms. Rosie move in to his home after learning of the treatment plan to target her particular type of cancer. From what she'd shared with me, she'd been wrecked by the chemo and was very grateful for her one and only child's devotion to help her.

Lately, she'd been making comments about finding her own place again, but the housing market in LA was absurd. I'd know. I shared a two-bedroom, one-bath apartment with my old college roommate because neither one of us could afford to live on our own income alone. Nora wanted to be an actress, and I wanted to make sure no actress got caught in a wig that looked more like roadkill than a million-dollar coiffure. Somehow our relationship continued to survive our nine-hundred-square-foot living space. But if she left an empty food package in the cabinets one more time instead of throwing it away, I'd need to pray the Holy Spirit intervened.

I punched the speaker button on the security box in front of the iron gate.

"Hey, Ms. Richards. Back so soon?" Kyle's voice sounded through the intercom.

"You know it," I called out.

Lamont Booker's security guard was a shameless flirt but completely harmless. He asked for my number every time I came by despite my assurances that I'd never fall for his charms. He was good-natured about being put in the friend zone—though could it be called that if I didn't actually consider us friends? More like work acquaintances?

The gate slid back into the stone wall, so I pulled forward onto the driveway, then waited for the gate to close behind my ancient MINI Cooper. Okay, not ancient, but a car made in 2010 might as well be. My parents gifted me the red hatchback as a high school graduation present. Since it still ran and the sunroof worked, I continued to drive it. And I would drive right on up to my high school reunion in it. But that was in a few weeks at the end of June and not my main concern.

After putting the car in park, I closed the sunroof. Sometimes my intense focus on the job caused me to forget to close the roof. I'd learned the hard way that seagull waste wasn't all that easy to get out of upholstery. Satisfied of its closure, I walked toward the hatchback to retrieve my supplies situated in my rolling stylist case. The all-black storage container looked like the old toy chests I'd seen in posts about the 1980s. My professional look, a nod to the '90s, came complete with a uniform consisting of black bib overalls that could perfectly hold hair clips and other various accessories. My dark blue tee would also conceal any water splashes.

I pulled my case behind me, heading for the lower-level garage entrance, where most of the help came in. After I pressed the buzzer, the door immediately swung open, and Kyle grinned at me. "Afternoon, beautiful." His gravelly voice held as much humor as the twinkle in his eyes.

"Hey, Kyle."

"Hey? That's it? Not, 'I missed you'?"

I placed a hand on my hip and a smirk on my lips. "Should I miss someone who doesn't sign my paychecks?"

"Ouch, girl." He clutched his muscled chest. "I thought we were better friends than that."

I laughed. "Not yet." I tossed a wave over my shoulder.

My rubber clogs fell silently on the light-colored wood floors as I traversed the hallway. The floor-to-ceiling windows let in copious amounts of sunshine. I sighed, thankful for the abundant light. I couldn't imagine living anywhere else in the world. Southern California held my heart.

The elevator entrance beckoned me. On my first day, Lamont Booker had taken one look at my styling case and shown me the boxed convenience. I'm not sure if he was concerned for his wood floors or genuinely worried that I couldn't lift the monstrosity up the stairs. Either way, I quickly became a fan of having an elevator in a house, as well as a tad bit envious, considering my entire apartment could fit into one of the rooms in this house, maybe even Ms. Rosie's closet.

Exiting the elevator, I made a right toward the mother-in-law suite. I rapped my knuckles on the door and heard a voice telling me to "Come in." Only darkness greeted me. Ms. Rosie lay in bed, her form hard to make out since the black-out blinds concealed all sources of natural light.

"Ms. Rosie?" I called softly.

Her face turned toward me, showing a furrowed brow and grimacing lips. "I'm so sorry, Nevaeh. I meant to cancel our appointment."

Her voice sounded thready to my ears. My stomach churned. "Are you okay? Should I go find your son?"

"No, please don't bother him." She tried to raise her arm, but it dropped limply onto her duvet cover.

"Does he know you're sick?" Was it the cancer? Had she relapsed? Did she need to go to the doctor? Get a scan or whatever it was medical professionals did to ensure cancer hadn't returned?

In all my time pampering Ms. Rosie, I'd never seen her look so bad. Then again, she'd canceled appointments before. Maybe moments like this had been the reason why.

"He does. It's just a stomach bug. I don't want you to get sick, too, so go." She turned her head the other way, a low moan filling the room.

I bit my lip. "I can make you some soup if he's not around. Is he on set?"

She nodded, groaning at the movement.

That was it. I couldn't leave her alone. "I'm making you some soup." From my understanding, Lamont Booker didn't have a personal chef. I think Ms. Rosie did most of the cooking, and she was in no position to make any meals today.

"You don't have to. I'll be fine," she murmured weakly.

Yeah, and I was the leading lady in the hottest new romantic comedy. Wait, no, that was Sandra Bullock. I had to give her two thumbs up for proving women in their fifties still had it. #Girlpower.

"It'll be no trouble. Promise." I slid a hand on my hip, trying to show my sass instead of the worry snaking through me.

"Thank you, Nevaeh."

"Anything for you, Ms. Rosie." I closed her door quietly, leaving my suitcase outside the entrance.

Ever since I'd first seen Lamont Booker's gorgeous kitchen with its white marble counters and double oven, I'd wanted to create a meal fit for a queen. And since the Sexiest Man Alive was a prince in Hollywood, his mom surely fit the bill.

I slid my hands along the ridiculously large island that could seat five people comfortably before opening the stainless-steel fridge. Organic fresh fruits and vegetables gleamed in their open containers while sparkling water and choice cuts of meat filled the shelves. Of course Mr. A-List wouldn't have anything highly processed. After walking through his huge pantry, I had a better idea of what I had to work with. Now to find the perfect recipe.

After perusing BonAPPetit on my phone, I found the perfect chicken-and-noodle soup that called for enough ginger and garlic to evict any germs from one's body. This kitchen had every appliance, but it was the gas range stove I wanted to get my hands on. I washed my hands, then got to laying out the ingredients.

Before long, a fragrant aroma filled the kitchen. While the soup simmered, I brought an herbal tea to Ms. Rosie's room. The thermometer confirmed she was fever-free, but she still looked pitiful in her dark room.

"Do you want me to open the blinds?"

"Please don't."

I wanted to argue, but who was I to dictate her environment when she was obviously under the weather? Back in the kitchen, I stirred the large pot with a wooden spoon. I reached for the egg noodles and—

"What are you doing?"

I yelped, and noodles flew everywhere.

Lamont Booker folded his arms over his impressive chest, glaring at the pasta scattered across his marble countertops.

"Why are you cooking in my house?" He glowered at the mess, as if the spilled food would have the answers to his questions.

"Ms. Rosie's sick, and she forgot to cancel our appointment. I couldn't just leave her here all alone, so I made soup." My words rushed out as I struggled for air.

His gaze rose to meet mine, and I drew in a ragged breath. Whew, I could see why *People* had dropped the coveted title on him.

"What do you mean she's sick?" Every word was elongated, making the question more pronounced.

I blinked. "You don't know? She told me you knew." She'd hoodwinked me!

"How sick?" he demanded.

I took a half step back. Lamont Booker intimidated me by just being *Lamont Booker*. This brooding, towering version made me want to hide behind the pantry door until he turned back into the swoony version I was used to seeing. But I wasn't one to cower, so I tilted my chin up. "She said it's just a stomach bug, but her blinds are closed, and she's lying in bed, obviously in pain."

He flew out of the kitchen, his footfalls pounding against the steps. I winced, then looked at the messy countertops. I found a dish rag and wiped up the pasta, then found a broom to take care of the pieces that had landed on the hardwood floor.

A few minutes later, he stalked back into the kitchen. I froze midsweep.

He stopped in front of the farmhouse sink and ran a hand over his bald head. "I'm sorry for startling you earlier."

"No problem. I was in my own world anyway." Dreaming of owning a place so luxurious. Wouldn't that show my parents that Nevaeh Richards wasn't *just* a stylist? They thought my career beneath me and the education they'd provided. Newsflash: I loved what I did. Even if it didn't live up to their standards or pay enough to get me a kitchen like Lamont Booker's.

"I appreciate you taking care of her. She said you've been checking in on her since you arrived."

"Of course." I dumped the food into the stainless-steel trash can, then put the broom back in the supply closet I'd rummaged through and rinsed out the rag I'd found to clean with.

"I added the noodles, so the soup will be ready in about five minutes. After that, you can pour her a bowl."

He opened his wallet, but I held up a hand. "I didn't do her hair, so you don't owe me anything."

"But you cooked. Cleaned too." He pointed to the gleaming countertops to emphasize his point.

"I don't charge people for helping them. That's just wrong." I blew out a breath. "Besides, the whole point of helping is doing without expecting something in return." I slid my hands into my pockets, wishing Lamont Booker had come home a little later—so late I could've given Ms. Rosie her soup and left unnoticed.

Other than the day he'd hired me and the time we spoke to discuss my fees, our conversations weren't the lengthy types. A greeting here or there. A nod in passing if he looked busy. We didn't normally just stand in his gorgeous kitchen and chat about his mother's health, unless it was hair-care related.

Now he stood before me in a white tee and gray joggers, and I wanted to swoon. Well, just a little. Okay, maybe enough to have a fangirl moment and ask if he'd sign something. Though what I didn't know. It's not like I carried paper around for such a thing. Although, living near Hollywood certainly afforded me opportunities for star sightings. But if I wanted to be taken seriously in this business, I couldn't go up to a celebrity and act uncouth.

"Then thank you very much for taking time to look after her." He smiled.

"Anytime." I walked out of the kitchen before I lost my composure. Surely, I had some kind of paper in my styling case that had space for a Lamont Booker signature.

"Oh, I saw your case upstairs. Let me grab that for you."

Right. I nodded. As soon as he was out of sight, I internalized a scream and fanned my face. Thank the Lord I didn't have to talk to that man on a regular basis. I was better than this. I saw A-list actors and celebrities all the time. Just the other day, I was behind one at a stop sign. I probably wouldn't have even realized it if it hadn't been for the vanity plate on his BMW.

The sound of pattering steps greeted my ears, and I blew out a breath. "Thanks for grabbing that." Time to exit stage left while my inner fan's mouth remained sealed with duct tape.

"Sure. I'll walk you out."

I barely kept my brow from rising. Since when did he walk me out? Was this when he'd lean in close and tell me never to step foot in his kitchen again? To leave his glorious gas range stove to him?

Instead, we walked in silence until he opened the front door. "Thanks again, Nevaeh."

"Of course. I hope Ms. Rosie feels better." Would it be impertinent for me to ask him to text me an update on her?

"Me too." For a moment, his mouth drew down and deep groves appeared, and my earlier thoughts on cancer returned, flooding my brain.

"She'll be okay, right?" I asked softly.

His gaze met mine, and he nodded. "She will."

I gulped and turned away. My foot slipped off the step that

had existed since the house was built, but apparently my brain had forgotten, despite the many times I'd stepped down before. My mouth opened to let out a panicked squeal, only a strong arm swooped around my stomach and tugged me close.

"You okay?" he murmured.

"Yeah," I breathed, heart hammering against my overalls.

He let me go, and my face heated as he lowered the suitcase. Obviously if I couldn't see a step, I couldn't drag a rolling suitcase behind me. Instead of thanking him for keeping my face from kissing the pavement, I pulled the handle up and walked away in embarrassment.

No wonder he was the Sexiest Man Alive. Even my pulse had reacted on instinct, and my stomach felt branded by his touch. Once again, I thanked God that I didn't have to see him on a daily basis. I'd be an absolute wreck.

One

My boss is so generous. She gave me three whole days to *look forward to* our meeting this morning. Isn't that just the sweetest, most considerate employer of all time? In my *anticipation*, I've spent the last seventy-two hours having no less than a dozen one-on-one's with her in my mind. After all, she never said what the meeting was in regard to, only that she wanted to talk to me about something important on Friday morning.

My mental scripts have ranged from approaching her office like a recalcitrant student about to be reprimanded by a stern principal (which isn't really fair, as Sofiya Bondaruk is more like Glinda the Good Witch in *The Wizard of Oz* than Ed Rooney from *Ferris Bueller's Day Off*) to the even more improbable scenario my housemate, coworker, and best friend, Keri, speculated—the promotion that always seems to take place around the holidays.

In the cases of extremes, the answer usually lies somewhere in the middle. I just haven't been able to figure out what that middle is, and it's spiking my anxiety.

The clock on my computer screen ticks off another minute. I take a deep breath and stand, my momentum pushing my rolling office chair a little too far out behind me. It crashes into the long table used as a second row of communal desks.

I flinch, heat blooming in my cheeks as if an invisible spotlight burns down on me. I duck my head so I don't have to see my coworkers staring over their MacBooks. If kryptonite is Superman's weakness, then being on the receiving end of the attention of others is mine. Even now, pinpricks of uncomfortable awareness press into my skin, as if Lincoln, Frank, and Rosa's gazes were needles that could actually pierce flesh.

Quietly, and as unobtrusively as I can, I push the chair back where it belongs and straighten my maroon sweater dress. Like it or not, it's time to face my boss and get this meeting over with.

The tips of my brown leather ankle boots bob in and out of my view of the polished concrete floor as I make my way from the industrial-sized main working space to Sofiya's office. I look up in the nick of time to avoid colliding with a pair of broad shoulders encased in a perfectly ironed button-up dress shirt. Even before the man with impeccable taste turns and looks down at me with brown eyes that have a ring of amber around the pupil, I know who the shoulders belong to.

Jeremy Fletcher.

Up close and personal.

A queer feeling twists low in my gut.

Usually, my glimpses of Jeremy are furtive. Quick secretive snatches no one sees that I tuck away to be pulled out in private. We've worked together for almost two years. Which means I've been pathetically pining over this elite specimen of a man for nearly as long. The same amount of time that he's barely been aware of my existence.

We've talked before, of course. If you count me barely squeaking out a *thank you* after he's opened the door for me as satisfactory interactions. But while I've hardly said more than two words to Jeremy in as many years, I've had innumerable conversations with him in my head. In those instances, I've always been impossibly witty, undeniably charming, and not the least bit tongue-tied.

So basically, my complete opposite in real life.

Jeremy tilts his head toward Sofiya's closed door. His layered brown hair sweeps in a perfect wave over his brow, every strand in place. I've read in books about heroines seeing a man's hair and wanting to run their fingers through it and tousle the strands. The idea seems almost like sacrilege to me. Jeremy is sculpted perfection. Why would I want to dishevel him?

He looks back at me and lowers his voice. "Know what this is about? Why Sofiya wants to see us?"

I open and close my mouth like a baby guppy. It's really not that hard to talk. Until you're put on the spot and someone is looking at you expectantly. My brain finds that too much pressure to function under.

The door swings open, and Sofiya stands on the other side, beaming at us with a glint in her eye.

If my boss wasn't the sweetest woman on the planet, I might be more scared of her. Forget every caricature of an office boss a la *The Devil Wears Prada* and think more along the lines of a Russian Cinderella. Tall and willowy with long light blond hair and skin like porcelain with a natural blush highlighting her prominent cheekbones. Even as Sofiya nears sixty-nine, her complexion is flawless. The kindness shining out of her pale blue eyes belies the inner strength I know she possesses.

"There you two are. Come in and sit down." She pivots and heads to her desk.

Jeremy moves to the side so I can enter the office first. I claim the seat on the left, and a moment later he lowers himself into the other chair on my right. It takes all my willpower, but

I keep my fingers from fidgeting on my lap. My eyes, however, don't know where to land. My gaze bounces around the office, catching first on a Better Business Bureau award nailed to the wall behind Sofiya's desk before flitting off to the layer of dust collected on the fake rubber plant in the corner.

Sofiya smiles warmly at us. "How are you two doing this morning?"

Oh yay. Small talk. My favorite.

I force a smile and say *good* even though my insides are twisted into a knot because I still haven't figured out what this meeting is about, even after three days of obsession.

Jeremy props an ankle over his opposite knee, physically relaxed and showing zero signs that he's worried about the outcome of the next few minutes. "It's been a crazy morning already, but that just means the day can only get better, right? What about you? Did you enjoy the orchestra last night?"

They go back and forth for a few minutes, conversation flowing comfortably between them while I wilt into the office chair's cushioned seat.

"So, you may be wondering why I requested a meeting this morning." Sofiya's words put immediate starch back in my spine.

Jeremy chuckles. "I was just asking Mackenzie that very thing when you opened the door."

Her eyes bounce to me, the curve of her lips suppressed to a smile instead of the wide grin it wants to be. I still, hoping she doesn't expect me to respond in any way.

With a small chuckle, Sofiya sits back. "Well, I won't make you wait any longer. The reason I wanted to talk to you both is because there's a new position opening up in the firm, and with the strengths you two individually bring to the table, I'm confident that either one of you would be an asset in the role. It's a supervisory position, but you both have shown leadership skills in the past. There will be more interaction with our clients than either of you may have experienced, but again, I think both of you are up to the task." She regards each of us in turn. "The hard part, really, is going to be deciding between you two for the job."

My lungs expel air. Keri was right? The last three days of worry were about a promotion? I guess I shouldn't have been so skeptical. I just didn't think I'd ever be a candidate. Not when I can't intelligibly talk to our clients outside of email. But the holiday season is always when employees move up at Limitless Designs.

And for reasons none of us can figure out, the person with the most Christmas cheer gets the advancement.

Every single time.

Sofiya extends her hand first to Jeremy and then to me. "I'll let you know my decision right after the holiday." Her phone rings, and she apologizes before answering.

I glance surreptitiously at Jeremy as he stands. Sofiya has effectively turned my secret office crush into my not-so-secret office rival. No doubt he is overjoyed by the possibility of a promotion. After all, that would be the normal reaction. The hollow pit in my stomach feels more like dread than joy, however.

It only takes that glance to prove what I already know: Jeremy Fletcher is put together, competent, and a shoe-in for this promotion. I am a hot mess and should throw in my red velvet Santa hat here and now.

Jeremy pauses once the office door is closed behind us. The sounds of our coworkers click-clacking away on their keyboards is the base soundtrack to most of my day and instantly brings me a sense of relief. As soon as I get back to my computer, I can bury my head in the proverbial sand of InDesign and finish the brochures for the Milwaukee Wilderness Group.

"Good luck," Jeremy says, his voice a rich timbre that doesn't hold even an ounce of mocking rivalry. Instead, he sounds . . . sincere.

I look up so I won't be talking to his middle button when I respond. I've never had a reason for such proximity before and have certainly never fabricated one. I'm more of the admire-from-afar type. Once upon a time, I'd have been considered a wallflower, which sounds so much better than the truth—that I'm still experiencing the shyness my parents swore I'd grow out of. Thirty-three years old and still waiting for a birthday to come around when I can unwrap the gift of not being awkward in social situations.

I open my mouth, but to my horror, an unintelligible sound slurs from my lips before I can clamp them closed.

Jeremy's brows pull low. But then the corner of his mouth quirks up. "See ya around, Mackenzie." He slips his fingers into his front pockets and strides away.

A flash of canary yellow enters my peripheral vision a second before Keri steps in front of me.

"Well?" she asks, eyes wide.

My shoulders slump. "I'm an idiot."

"Don't talk about my best friend that way." She plants her hands on her hips.

"Even if it's true?"

"Lies!"

I look over Keri's shoulder as Jeremy turns the corner, disappearing from view. This isn't the first impression I've made on Jeremy, but before, I could take comfort in knowing I'd presented myself with quiet professionalism. I was okay with my position of nameless coworker, feeding my hidden feelings without any real-life interaction. But now everything has changed.

Keri hooks her arm through mine and tugs. "Stairwell. Now."

Since our office is on the ninth floor, no one takes the stairs. That abandoned corner of the building has become our echoey space when we need a few stolen moments and don't want to be overheard.

Keri pushes on the metal exit bar to open the heavy door to the stairs. The air is cooler, with no heat circulating the small but tall space. The latch clicks behind us, and Keri twirls, the yellow skirt of her vintage dress spiraling out over her petticoats. I told her once she reminds me of Mary Tyler Moore from *The Dick Van Dyke Show*, and she'd given me a beaming smile.

"Tell me everything."

I sigh and sit on the top stair heading down to the eighth floor. Keri gathers her skirts and gingerly settles next to me.

"Jeremy Fletcher and I are officially competing for the same promotion."

She nudges my shoulder with hers. "This is good news, Kenz. You should be celebrating, not looking like your cat just died. You know what you have to do to win the promotion. You're practically an honorary elf, so this will be easy for you."

But my favorite parts of Christmas are the secret Santa parts. Emphasis on *secret*. I can crank up Mariah Carey or Nat King Cole and rock out to them in my car. Bake dozens of sugar cookies and gingerbread men and drop them off at my neighbor's in-house daycare for the children to decorate. Fill up the Toys for Tots bin at the store and imagine a marine in uniform making a kid's day on Christmas morning. Build a snowman in the memory care facility's yard.

None of these things require me to speak to multiple people or draw any sort of attention to myself.

Christmas should be twinkle lights and snowflake kisses. Magic sprinkled in the air like sugar on holiday cookies. The spirit of the season is supposed to work like a Magic Eraser on the stresses and doldrums of everyday life. It's the something special that happens when Jack Frost nips at your nose and when the nostalgia of music played only one time of year harmonizes with the Salvation Army bell ringers to bring a perfect pitch to the world's favorite holiday.

But instead of a Hallmark Channel marathon of festive magic, Sofiya is taking something good and joyous and making it into her own production of *Christmas Wars: Office Edition.*

"Have you ever wondered why Sofiya always does promotions around the holidays and then awards the job to the person with the most Christmas spirit?" Keri's accustomed to carrying more than her fair share of the conversation. It's one of the reasons we're such good friends. "I mean, the first year, I thought it was merely a coincidence. But it keeps happening. It's turned into a competition for who can out-Christmas the other person, not necessarily who is better for the job."

"I think it has something to do with her childhood."

Keri looks at me, her bright red lips perched to the side. "What do you mean?"

I pick my words carefully. Too many times I've said something and the meaning came across differently than I intended. "Well, she's kind of like the Grinch."

Keri's forehead scrunches. "But Sofiya is the sweetest. She loves Christmas more than anyone I know."

See? "You're right. She's the best. I didn't mean she's the Grinch because she's grumpy. More like . . ." I pause, searching. "They share a similar history."

She considers this. "I'm not sure I know the Grinch's backstory. Just that he's a mean one, he's a heel, and you don't want to touch him with a thirty-nine-and-a-half-foot pole. Oh, and his heart grows three sizes."

I smile at her. "Well, in the book, no one knows why he has a grudge against Christmas, just that all the carolers and merrymaking and joy are a trigger that sets off his holiday hatred. The movies have attempted to fill in the gap with a tragic tale of an unwanted orphan, abandoned, just wanting to be loved and accepted. Christmas became the symbol of his rejection and loneliness, especially backlit by everyone else's family celebrations and happiness."

She taps her fingers on her knee. "Okay, I'm following. Keep going."

"The Grinch tried to steal everyone's holiday so they could experience the emptiness he felt growing up, while Sofiya—"

Understanding dawns in Keri's expression. "Sofiya overcompensates the lack of Christmas joy in her past by rewarding those who can fill that void." She leans in, whispering even though we are the only two people in the stairwell. "Do you think she even knows she's doing it?"

Maybe other bosses manipulated their employees for personal reasons, but not Sofiya. "She's probably operating on a subconscious level."

"Are you going to talk to her about it?"

That doesn't deserve a response. I give Keri a look I know she can decipher.

"Right. Awkward conversations. What was I thinking?"

Keri doesn't get it because she has no problem talking to anyone. Meanwhile, I'd rather spend three hours Googling the answer to a question than three minutes on the phone asking the same question.

"I think I'll just bow out. Jeremy deserves the promotion, plus he'll do a better job than I would. The position requires leadership skills and direct communication with our clients. I'd probably lose the company more accounts than anything. You know how I am."

Keri lays a hand on my arm. "Mackenzie, you can't quit."

"Not quit, just not jump through Sofiya's hoops."

197

"You might not have a choice." She holds my gaze, her eyes round and soft. She reaches into a deep side pocket, pulling out an envelope, which she gives me.

I look down at the white rectangle in my hand, recognizing the return address immediately as Heritage Hills. My palms grow sweaty, and I fumble with the seal.

"I checked the mail slot this morning before we left," Keri explains, "but I didn't want any bad news to cloud your head before your meeting, so I held on to it."

I flip open the paper and read, my stomach dropping. "Her insurance won't cover as much as I hoped. Keri, I can't afford my mom's care."

She squeezes my arm. "You can if you get the promotion. It comes with a significant raise. I saw the budget proposal myself."

I sigh as my heart plummets. Whether I like it or not, I have no choice but to play Sofiya's reindeer games.

Toni Shiloh is a wife, a mom, and an award-winning Christian contemporary romance author. She writes to bring God glory and to learn more about His goodness. Her novel *In Search of a Prince* won the first ever Christy Amplify Award. *Grace Restored* was a 2019 Holt Medallion finalist, *Risking Love* was a 2020 Selah Award finalist, *The Truth about Fame* a 2021 Holt Medallion finalist, and *The Price of Dreams* a 2021 Maggie Award finalist. A member of American Christian Fiction Writers (ACFW), Toni loves connecting with readers and authors alike via social media. You can learn more about her writing at tonishiloh.com.

Sign Up for
Toni's Newsletter

Keep up to date with Toni's latest news on book releases and events by signing up for her email list at the link below.

FOLLOW TONI ON SOCIAL MEDIA

Toni Shiloh, Author   @tonishiloh   @tonishilohwrite

ToniShiloh.com

More from Toni Shiloh

Hollywood hair stylist Neveah loves making those in the spotlight shine. But when a photo of her and Hollywood heartthrob Lamont goes viral for all the wrong reasons, they suddenly find themselves in a fake relationship to save their careers. In a world where nothing seems real, can Neveah be true to herself . . . and her heart?

The Love Script

Fashion aficionado Iris Blakely dreams of using her talent to start a business to help citizens in impoverished areas. But when she discovers that Ekon Diallo will be her business consultant, the battle between her desires and reality begins. Can she keep her heart—and business—intact despite the challenges she faces?

To Win a Prince

Brielle Adebayo's simple life unravels when she discovers she is a princess in the African kingdom of Qlqrǫ Ilé and must immediately assume her royal position. Brielle comes to love the island's culture and studies the language with her handsome tutor. But when her political rivals force her to make a difficult choice, a wrong decision could change her life.

In Search of a Prince